Renegade Boys 3

Lock Down Publications and Ca$h
Presents
Renegade Boys 3
A Novel by *Meesha*

Lock Down Publications
P.O. Box 870494
Mesquite, Tx 75187

Visit our website @
www.lockdownpublications.com

Copyright 2019 by Meesha
Renegade Boys 3

First Edition September 2019
Printed in the United States of America

This is a work of fiction. Names, characters, places, and incidents either are products of the author's imagination or are used fictitiously. Any similarity to actual events or locales or persons, living or dead, is entirely coincidental.

Lock Down Publications
Like our page on Facebook: Lock Down Publications @
www.facebook.com/lockdownpublications.ldp
Cover design and layout by: **Dynasty Cover Me**
Book interior design by: **Shawn Walker**
Edited by: **Tam Jernigan**

Stay Connected with Us!

Text **LOCKDOWN** to 22828 to stay up-to-date with new releases, sneak peaks, contests and more…

Thank you.

Submission Guideline.

Submit the first three chapters of your completed manuscript to ldpsubmissions@gmail.com, subject line: Your book's title. The manuscript must be in a .doc file and sent as an attachment. Document should be in Times New Roman, double spaced and in size 12 font. Also, provide your synopsis and full contact information. If sending multiple submissions, they must each be in a separate email.

Have a story but no way to send it electronically? You can still submit to LDP/Ca$h Presents. Send in the first three chapters, written or typed, of your completed manuscript to:

LDP: Submissions Dept
Po Box 870494
Mesquite, Tx 75187

DO NOT send original manuscript. Must be a duplicate.

Provide your synopsis and a cover letter containing your full contact information.

Thanks for considering LDP and Ca$h Presents.

Meesha

Chapter 1
Shake

Sitting around the corner from the funeral home where that nigga Max's service was taking place, I was waiting for the call to put Big Jim's plan into play. Rod was the only one out of the crew that could go to the service without suspicion. The plan was to fall in line with the funeral possession to the cemetery, wait for them to lower the casket, and light that bitch up. Whoever got hit, was on them. Ricio and Sosa fucked with the wrong muthafuckas and had to pay. My phone rang and I knew it was showtime.

"Yeah," I said into the phone.

"In about five minutes or so, the line will start moving. They're lining up now, be ready."

The line went dead and I got out of the car to let the other's in on what was going down. I didn't know why Floyd wasn't here but I was ready to show Big Jim that I was capable of holding shit down without his scary ass sidekick. There was something off about his ass lately anyway and I could foresee his downfall.

"Aye, Rod just called and said they were lining up. We will fall in line after the last car with an orange sticker in the window. When the casket starts lowering into the ground, start blasting. It's time to get back at them for every one of the soldiers that died by their hands. Don't show no mercy for nobody! Get in position," I barked.

There were three cars that were riding with me on this mission. The niggas from the Southside were savages and I should've been rolling with them instead of the pussy muthafuckas I had been dealing with. Shit, half of them were eating mud burgers because they were too busy not paying attention in the middle of a war. I went back to the car and told Boogie to drive because I wanted to make my tool clap without worrying about peeling out afterwards.

A few minutes passed before the hearse came rolling down the street. The line was long as hell and it seemed like it took forever to get to the end. I didn't know Max knew so many people but a lot of them came out to send him off. Rello pulled out first, I instructed

Boogie to go next, and Erv brought up the rear. There was nine of us in total and we were locked and loaded.

It took about thirty minutes to get to the cemetery and the shit brought my adrenaline down a few notches. I had a few homies that were laying in the very cemetery that I was about to disrupt, but I had to push all that to the back of my mind for another day. The line finally stopped at what would be Max's final resting place.

Watching people exit their cars as Ricio, Sosa, and many other men headed to the hearse, I lit a blunt. The sight of the two of them had my blood racing. It took everything in me not to start busting at their asses then, but I was going to let them get their brother settled first. There were some niggas I had never seen before looking around like they were secret service agents and shit, but they wouldn't be able to defend what they didn't see coming.

I picked up my phone and called Rello and Erv. "Follow my lead. When the casket starts lowering and the people start walking off, go. Spray that muthafucka and hit whatever's in the way!" I said hanging up.

The casket was being carried over to the grave that was dug for this occasion and my palms started sweating. I'd been waiting to get back at these niggas for weeks and I was finally about to get my chance. The preacher had everyone bow their heads for what was more than likely a prayer. That would've been the perfect opportunity to attack but with my delayed reaction, I missed it. They released a bunch of birds after the prayer and the casket started lowering. That was my cue.

"Go!" I yelled at Boogie.

He pressed on the gas, swerving from behind the line of cars. I sat on the edge of the window sill and aimed my nine-millimeter out of the window. Rello and Erv rode over graves in different directions and I let off the first round of shots. People scrambled for cover and in a matter of seconds, it looked like a war zone in the middle of the cemetery. Boogie jumped from the car, using it as a shield. His .45 magnum was rocking like a rap song and it was music to my ears.

I unloaded my clip and snatched my .357 from my hip. A pretty bitch was busting at my ass like Lara Croft and a bullet whizzed past my head as I ducked down in the seat. Boogie ran from behind the car and got knocked instantly. Firing out of the window, I hit the bitch in the chest with two slugs and jumped into the driver's seat. Tez and Ro jumped in the car before I peeled off.

Bullets were still flying in our direction as I fled the scene. The side window exploded and Ro howled out in pain. The sound that came from his mouth told me he had been hit. I looked into the review mirror and Tez was taking his shirt off.

"How bad is it?" I asked flying southbound on Kedzie Avenue.

"It's bad, my nigga! He got a big ass hole in his chest! We need to get him to a hospital! Ro, look at me! Keep ya eyes open!" Tez screamed in a panic.

"Calm yo ass down and keep pressure on his chest. There's a hospital on 129th, we should be there in about five minutes or so," I told him.

I fumbled for my phone to call to see where Erv and Rello was. Speeding through a red light as I continued on Kedzie, Boom! The phone fell from my hand and my head hit the steering wheel as the car swerved to the left into ongoing traffic. I whipped the car back to the right with blurred vision. A black SUV was coming up behind me fast and I knew whoever was in that truck was about to ram me again. I floored the gas pedal and sped down the street.

"We losing him. Shake! Tez screamed.

"He gon' die because them niggas is on our ass and stopping is not an option! As a matter of fact, shoot out the tires!" Tez was hesitant about letting up on the pressure he was putting on Ro's wound. "Let that shit go and start bustin' at them niggas!" I barked staring at him through the rearview mirror.

Doing as I instructed, he leaned out the window and starting shooting but that didn't stop the truck from ramming us again. I turned left on 127th barely missing a car that was coming through the light. The truck came through behind me and bullets came flying through the back window. Tez was trying his best to shoot back but he was outnumbered.

Meesha

"Get in the right lane and floor this muthafucka, Shake!" Tez yelled.

I was weaving in and out of traffic and clipped a parked car. I lost control and hit the median. I tried my best to avoid the light pole but I couldn't. The impact was fierce and the Impala damn near wrapped around it. My head hit the window hard and all I could hear was the sound of the tires spinning because I couldn't take my foot off the gas pedal.

"Tez! Tez!" I called out as blood ran in my eyes. He didn't respond and I couldn't check to see if he was dead or alive. I had so much blood running down my face and it was dripping on my arm and down the front of my shirt.

I heard footsteps approaching fast in my direction. I couldn't do anything but sit there and wait for whatever was going to happen. I laid still with my eyes closed, pretending to be dead. Whoever it was came up to the car and started shooting inside. I was hit in the arm, my side and in my back. The burning sensation felt like somebody was sticking hot coals all over my body. It had to be by the grace of God that I didn't get hit more times than I did.

"This is for Max, pussy muthafucka!" was shouted with one final shot to my chest. The screeching of tires was all I remembered hearing before I lost consciousness.

"I don't think there are any survivors," I heard a voice say as I struggled to open my eyes.

"The ambulance is on its way. I know for a fact the two in the back are gone."

The wailing of the ambulance was close but I didn't know how much longer I would be able to hold on. My eyes were stuck together by the blood that oozed from my head. "Aaaagh!" I screamed out as I tried to move.

"Don't move, man! The ambulance is coming down the street now," a man said through the window. "You won't be able to get yourself out. The firemen are here to cut you out."

"Move back, sir," one of firemen said to the man. "Was he communicating with you?"

"Yes, he's conscious now but he wasn't before you all got here. There are two in the back seat and I don't think they made it," the man explained.

"Okay, thank you so much. Let's get the Jaws of Life and get this guy out of this car."

A few moments later, there was a loud noise and the sound of metal being forced opened. "It appears his leg is trapped under the dash. We'll have to cut the top off and use the ram to push the dash out to free him."

"Whatever we have to do, we must do it now. He's lost a lot of blood and needs medical attention immediately. The paramedics can't do anything while he's in this car."

The firefighters got to work and had the roof of the car pushed back in a matter of minutes. I could see the sky through the small slit of my eyes and I could feel the slight wind on my face. The machine started back up and the pressure on my leg was easing with every push to the dash board. I couldn't move and the pain was unbearable.

"Get him out! The other two are deceased, we will let the coroner deal with that situation."

Someone I presumed was a paramedic, stabilized my leg and started cutting my shirt off my body. "He has several gunshot wounds, and there's a laceration on his forehead. We have to get him on a stretcher!"

When the paramedics, with the help of the firemen, got me out of the car, I laid as still as possible just in case the people that did this were still around. Lifting me into the ambulance, the paramedics started an IV and put an oxygen mask over my face. I was losing consciousness while thinking about how I was going to kill Sosa and Ricio.

Meesha

Chapter 2
Beast

"Sin!" I raced over to where she had fallen and heard cars peeling out of the cemetery. "Get them muthafuckas!" I screamed as I ran to see about Sin.

Falling to my knees, I was in full combat mode but this time it was different. It wasn't one of my comrades I was trying to save, it was the love of my life. Being careful not to move her, I checked for a pulse and found one. It didn't stop my heart from pounding in my ears because I was looking for blood and couldn't find any.

"Please baby, I hope you were smart this morning," I whispered softly. Snatching her jacket open and lifting her shirt, I closed my eyes and my head dropped. "That's why you my bitch!"

I thanked God that Sin had put her vest on under her shirt. It was custom made for shit like this and I was glad I'd made the investment. There were two slugs stuck in the vest directly in the heart area. If she hadn't been protected, we would be planning her funeral next.

"Sin," I said her name while tapping her lightly on the face. "Come on baby, look at me," I said softly.

She slowly started coming to and I let out a sigh of relief. As her eyes fluttered open, I kissed her on the lips and brought her body to an upright position and held her tightly. Sin was alert and had the look of revenge written on her face. Ricio and Sosa came over, kneeling down to check on her.

"We got to go, a news van pulled into the cemetery as Alejandro and the rest of the Vasquez clan went after them niggas. I don't know how the fuck they knew about what happened so fast," Ricio said.

As soon as he told me about the news van, I saw a reporter and the cameraman get out of their truck to set up for their false story. Wasn't shit to report because everybody that got hurt was already gone. Sosa jumped up and stomped in their direction. "Sosa, don't go over there!" I yelled at his back.

He stopped suddenly and turned around with those jet-black eyes, "Sosa is back in the box. These muthafuckas brought hell back to the city. They want a war, that's what the fuck they gon' get. I'm not going back in until everyone of them are eating dirt, that includes Big Jim," he said walking fast towards the reporter.

"Ricio, go stop him!" I said sternly.

"Let him go, I agree with him this time. They shot me and ain't shit gon' stop me from going after them. Don't try to talk me out of it because you are included in the 'them' I'm talking about if your ass starts talking shit," Sin said getting up and pulling off her jacket.

She took off her vest like it was a bra, without taking her shirt off. I never understood how women did that shit but I was fascinated by it every time I saw it done. As Sin examined the slugs that were stuck in the vest, steam was coming out of her ears.

"Sin, I don't want you to do anything without consulting with me first," I said glaring at her.

"Did them pussy muthafuckas consult with you before they shot me? Hell nawl, they didn't! That's not how this street shit work, I'm getting at their ass the same way they tried to get at me! I'm Sin City and I'm not signing no fuckin' permission slip to slump a nigga! You got me all the way fucked up, Beast," she said tossing the vest at me and walking over to Madysen.

I'd forgotten all about Madysen but it was a good thing Nija and her girl Kimmie was there to comfort her. Ricio walked over to Max's grave and looked down into the hole. His lips were moving but I couldn't hear what he was saying. One of the cemetery workers came over and Ricio stood after dropping something in the hole.

"Aye, I'm staying right here until y'all put that vault lid in place and cover my brother up,"

"We're on break and will get to it in about an hour," the guy said turning to walk away.

"Nah, fuck yo' break! You about to do this shit now! You on my time right now, what I say is law! If you don't want to make it happen, I'll put yo' ass down there with him and cover this bitch myself! This ain't the time to test my gangsta. Move!"

The guy went over to the other workers and they all moved fast, doing what Ricio instructed. Shaking my head, I noticed Rodrigo was talking into the mic like he was giving a press conference or something across the cemetery. Nothing good was going to come from whatever the fuck he was up to.

"What the hell is yo' brother doing?" I asked Ricio.

Looking over his shoulder, "Ain't no telling, that nigga ain't himself once again. Rodrigo don't give a fuck about nothing," Ricio said turning back around.

"Aye y'all, I'm about to go handle this business," Psycho said walking up.

"What business is that?" Ricio asked.

"I'm going to holla at Rod. It's not sitting well with me that he saw me at the funeral home and didn't give me a heads up about what Floyd had planned. Don't think I didn't see that black Impala, you say it belongs to him, I will dig into that. You know what fucked me up? That nigga knew I was here with y'all, and he let them muthafuckas air this bitch out! Rod showed he ain't got no love for me!" Psycho said punching his hand.

"Go handle yo' business but be careful, Psych. Ease into that shit, he's looking for you to come at him wrong. I need you to act like a lame ass nigga, get in his head, and act clueless. Make him think you need him, then go in hard. Don't hesitate to hit us up if you need assistance," Ricio said shaking up with him.

"Psycho, I know that's your father, don't allow him to sell you a dream. There's no way in hell he should still have breath in his body after today," I said looking him in his eyes.

"Beast, he ain't no father of mine! What type of father sits back and uses his son as target practice? I don't have no love for that nigga! He's already dead to me! I'm out," he said heading to his car.

Psycho had a point. I was glad Rod set the tone in a way his son could see for himself what type of nigga he really was. Sin was who I was worried about because it was going to be hard to keep up with her. Looking over to where Sin and the other ladies were, Madysen was bawling her eyes out and Nija was trying to calm her down. I walked over and stooped down in front of her.

"Madysen, come on and get up. I know you are scared but everything will be okay. Are you hurt?" I asked calmly.

"Beast, why would they come here shooting while we were trying to bury Max?" She wailed. "Wasn't it enough that they killed him?"

"Calm down, Mads. No one got hurt. You know what's going on and it won't stop until we finish this shit. I don't want you to worry about any of this, all you have to do is take care of yourself and bring the baby into the world healthy."

"I just want everything to be over, Beast. Why didn't one of those bullets hit me?" she screamed.

"Bitch, if you don't shut yo' stupid ass up! A bullet didn't hit yo' ass because God didn't see fit to take your selfish ass to his plush island because it's not your time! If you really want to die, I'll do the job myself once you drop that load," Sin said as she glared at Madysen.

"Sin—"

"I don't want to hear it, Erique," she said cutting me off. "She's feeding off the fact that you are going to coddle her ass like a two-year-old. It's time for her to woman up and stop acting like the shit that's happening is affecting only her. I just got shot twice in the chest and could've died, do you see me sitting back whining about it? Get your shit together Madysen, this is not the time to fuck with me," Sin said walking over to Max's grave.

When Sin City is present, we bumped heads like a muthafucka. I saw nothing but battles ahead between us. In her mind, she had a dick bigger than mine and seemed to forget who the fuck I was. I was going to let that shit slide because I wasn't in the right frame of mind to talk to her.

"I want you to stop talking nonsense, Mads. It's hard to think positive at a time like this but I'm gon' need you to push harder to move forward. Max wouldn't want you to be sad at all. He is smiling down on you waiting on you to smile again. No one can tell you how to grieve, but we all will definitely do all we can to keep you happy through this time. Come on, get up and I'll walk you to the car," I said with my hand held out.

Madysen let me help her up. "I'll go sit in the car, thank you for caring about me. That's more than I can say about others," she said walking off.

I was glad Sin didn't hear what she said. At that point, I'm sure I wouldn't have been able to stop whatever happened. Once Madysen was safely inside my car, I turned as Nija stood up and brushed off the back of her pants. I looked at her and motioned toward Ricio. She looked at me confused. "What are you trying to say, Beast?" she asked.

"Go talk to him, Nija."

Shaking her head, "I don't have anything to say to him. I got him through the funeral like I promised, my job is done. One of his many female friends can console him because I'm not. If you need me to help with Madysen in any way, give me a call. I don't have a problem with helping to cheer her up. I'm out of here, "Nija said giving me a hug.

"I hear what you're saying, Nija. Think about it, okay?" I said stepping out of her embrace.

"There's nothing to think about, I've made up my mind. Ricio has to decide what his intentions are when it comes to me. I need a man that will love me and only me. I know my worth and I've allowed him to do him far too long. It's my time to live life for me," she said backing away.

There was nothing I could say because she was right. For her to be young, she was wise beyond her years. Ricio was losing a good girl and I was sure she was going to stand on her words. I glanced over to Max's gravesite and he was still grilling the workers as they filled the hole.

"Okay, Nija. I'll see you later," Sin said walking over to give her a hug. "Thanks for coming and be careful out here. Call me when you get to your destination."

"Will do. There's no need to thank me for coming. Max was my brother and I wouldn't have missed his homegoing for anything in the world. Keep an eye on Ricio, Sin."

"I got both of those knuckleheads. Take care of yourself and call me anytime."

Nija nodded her head before turning around to walk away. Kimmie waved goodbye and followed behind her. I watched as they got closer to Nija's car and Ricio rushed past me taking huge steps to catch Nija before she got in her vehicle.

"Nija!" he yelled out.

She ignored him and kept going. Opening the car door, Nija got in and closed the door. Kimmie got in on the passenger side as the engine roared to life. Ricio made it to the car in record time. Nija was looking up at Ricio and his lips were moving a mile a minute.

"He fucked up a good thing," Sin said walking up to me.

"Yeah, I think he did," was the only thing I could say. Watching the cemetery workers dump the last pile of dirt on Max's grave, I searched the grounds for Rodrigo. "Where the hell is that damn Rodrigo?" I asked Sin.

"He's sitting in his car. I don't know what the hell he said to those reporters because they hauled ass out of here like their lives depended on it," Sin laughed.

"Sin, that shit is not funny. Nine times out of ten, whatever he did was on live tv!" I said shaking my head. Come on so we can get out of here." We walked in the direction of my car and I stopped grabbing her hand. "Don't say anything to Madysen, please."

"Man, fuck that lil girl! She is your problem, Beast. I will not raise my blood pressure over a muthafucka that don't give a damn about herself or her unborn child. Stop coming at me about her too. From this point on, I will act like her ass don't exist until she gets her mind right," she said walking ahead of me to the car.

Ricio was coming my way and I watched Nija drive off. I met him halfway and his phone chimed on his hip. He snatched it off and looked up at me, "Alejandro wants to meet at my crib, they were able to get at them niggas in one of the cars. You following me or what?" he asked.

"Nah, I'll roll out with you. Let me tell Sin what's going on and I'll meet you at your ride."

"Aight, bet. I'll text Rodrigo and let him know the plan."

I knew Sin was about to talk shit, but she was taking her ass home to lay the fuck down. Going around to the passenger window

18

I leaned on the window sill. "Aye, we have some business to attend to and I want you to go home. I'll be there as soon as I can."

"I'm going too—"

"Negative! You will go home, Sin. We will take care of this," I said cutting her off. "You were shot in the fuckin' chest and by the grace of God, you were not hurt!"

"It was my quick thinking that saved my fuckin' life! I have every right to go after these punks, Beast! You know what, I'll go home but I'm letting you know right now, you won't be able to stop my movements for long," she said climbing over the console.

Sin pushed the start button and put the car in drive. I moved back without responding to what she'd said. There were other issues that needed to be handled and her feelings weren't one of them. I watched my car until it was out of sight, then I jumped in the car with Ricio.

Meesha

Chapter 3
Psycho

Doing over ninety miles an hour on the expressway, I was fuming. Rod had a lot of explaining to do. It didn't matter that he was my father, I was going to bust his shit if he lied. He put me out of the house because of my dealings in the street and his ass was in it just as deep as I was. Look at the pot calling the kettle black.

Thoughts were flooding my mind and I couldn't keep up with them. One thought in particular was why my mother up and left us out of the blue. Those were questions he was going to answer even if he didn't want to. He was a lawyer and made good damn money but, he was knee deep in the game. Why though?

The thing that got me was the fact he put me of all people in a bad situation back at the cemetery. I wasn't his son when he sent them niggas to shoot up the burial, I was another muthafucka who was stepping on Big Jim's toes. His loyalty was to them, not me. Those feelings alone were the reason Rodney Banks was going to die by my hands.

Signaling to get over so I could exit the expressway, I slowed down because the Chicago police was always on bullshit. As I entered the neighborhood where I was raised, all the good times came to mind. Being the only child had its perks and cons. My parents were very protective of me and I couldn't do much of anything. The only thing I was able to do was go to school and back home.

I met Ricio at Simeon high school and we played basketball together and a brotherhood began. Reese welcomed me with open arms and treated me like one of his own. Their house was where I spent majority of my time and my father didn't like it. I didn't know why until all this shit came out.

Cruising down Marquette Road, I started getting mad all over again the closer I got to Ashland Avenue. I made a left on 65th street heading toward Honore Street. I parked down the street from my childhood home and fired up a blunt. I didn't see the nigga's car when I passed the house, so I knew he wasn't in the crib, but I still had a key. After finishing my blunt, I got out and walked to the crib and climbed the stairs.

Inserting the key that I've had for years into the lock, it didn't turn. His ass changed the fuckin' locks and didn't even say shit. It wasn't going to stop me from getting inside though. I walked to the side of the house and went to the basement door. Lifting the glass slowly, I stuck my hand inside and unlocked the door. That was my way of sneaking in when I was younger, I guess he still didn't know about it because it wasn't fixed.

I made my way up the stairs and started looking around the house. There was nothing out of place that I could tell. One thing I did notice was the fact that there was no indication of him having a family. There were no pictures of me nor my mama anywhere. It made me feel like he cut me completely out of his life. Sitting in the comfy chair facing the door, I placed my nine-millimeter on my lap and waited for Rod to come home.

Passing time by scrolling social media and watching sports on my phone, I checked the time. It was damn near six o'clock and he still hadn't showed up. The thought of leaving was in the forefront of my mind but I didn't know if this opportunity would come this smoothly again. Thirty minutes later I stood to leave and I heard a car door slam. I sat back down when I heard the sound of keys jingling on the other side of the door.

The blinds were closed so the room was semi dark. I placed my gun between the cushion of the chair. Rod walked inside and locked the door behind him before hitting the light switch on the wall. When he turned around, he let out a low gasp with his hand to his chest.

"How the fuck did you get in my house? I changed the locks for a reason!" Rod barked.

"I came through the basement. This was the first place I thought to come after what happened at the cemetery."

Rod shifted from one foot to the other nervously. I was trying not to snap and give him the opportunity to tell me he knew about what went down. "What happened?" he asked walking slowly to the sofa and sat down.

"Some niggas came through and aired out the site. The shit was foul as fuck and I know Floyd and his cronies are behind it!"

"How do you figure that, Pierre?"

"Come on, man! You a street nigga! Don't call me that shit, my name is Psycho!"

"I don't care what they call you in the streets, you were named Pierre and that's what I'll continue to call you," he said properly. "I've never been in these streets so I don't know how you let that come out of your mouth. You were raised to be a man not one of these street thugs! It was your choice to go another route, son. I wanted you to be a lawyer like me!"

Chuckling at his comical ass, I looked him in the eyes and leaned forward with my elbows on my knees. "You wanted me to be a lawyer but I turned out to be a street nigga like you huh, Rod."

"Rod, who the fuck is that?"

"Yo' ass! You didn't think I would ever find out about your double life, *Rod*?"

"My name is Rodney Pierre Banks! I'm a successful attorney, nothing more, nothing less! I've never been any kind of street nigga!"

I was hitting a nerve because he was becoming irater with every word he spoke. The vein in the middle of his forehead was protruding. He had a scowl on his face like he was ready to kill my ass. It was funny because he thought he was scaring a nigga.

"Big Jim calls yo' ass Rod, nigga! You own the black Impala that was used the night Reese was killed and it was the same muthafuckin' ride that shot up the burial today! I spoke to you at the funeral home and you let me go to that cemetery blind without telling me what was going down! I could've been killed today and you didn't give a fuck!" I said standing to my feet.

"I didn't know shit about any of that! I haven't owned an impala in years and it damn sure wasn't black!" he screamed jumping up. "I don't know shit about Big Jim except he's a big-time drug dealer that's serving time in prison where he needs to be."

While he was talking his shit, I was texting Beast to get some information to throw at his punk ass. I was done playing with Rod's ass and I was getting closer to killing him, I just needed him to get madder to get more out of him. I started pacing back and forth while shaking my head.

"I don't know who told you these things and added my name to the mix, but I know it's false. I have never associated myself with filth. I'm ashamed that my son was out in the street slinging dope, while I stood in courtrooms putting dealers behind bars!" My phone chimed and a picture message came through with the information I needed. I looked up at Rod and grinned.

"Fuck that political shit you talking! Let's speak on the fact that you said you didn't own a black Impala. In my hand I hold proof that you in fact owned a 2014 black Impala, license plate number ROD 7414!" I said walking across the room to show him the picture. "Ain't this you back in the day flexing next to the car you lied about having?" I asked swiping to the next picture that Beast sent. "This document states that you are the muthafucka that's representing James Carter better known as Big Jim in his murder case. You stood in my face and told a bold-faced lie, *Rod*!"

"I—I—that's not true!" he yelled trying to snatch my phone out of my hand.

Pushing him back, I hit him in his jaw and dropped his punk ass. One thing I despised was a lying ass nigga. I didn't give a fuck about him being my father because he was an op at that moment. He didn't give a fuck about me and I didn't give a fuck about him either.

"You wanted me to die today, muthafucka! You had a chance to tell me that my head was on a platter going to that cemetery but you didn't say shit!" I kicked him in his ribcage and he balled up in a fetal position. "Get the fuck up, Rod!" He laid there without getting up so I kicked his ass again. Snatching him up by the collar of his shirt, I slung him onto the sofa and kneeled in front of him.

"You gon' stop lying now? I don't want to hear nothing but the truth. I already know you killed Reese, work for Big Jim legally and illegally, and you had a hand in them niggas trying to kill us today. Tell me something I don't know, *Rod*."

"I didn't send nobody to do shit!" he screamed in my face.

Standing to my feet, I drew my fist back and knocked the slob out of his mouth. "This is not the time for you to play the tough cookie role, nigga. You are seconds away from taking your last breath," I said turning my back on him.

I walked slowly to the chair and grabbed my piece. Taking the silencer out of my pocket, I screwed it onto the nozzle. Regret was trying to creep into my mind but I pushed that shit out swiftly. He may be my father but betrayal from anyone is malicious, no matter the bloodline connection.

"What is the plan, Rod?" I asked turning around with my finger on the trigga.

His eyes bulged when he saw the gun at my side. Rod threw his hands above his head and stood up. "Sit yo' ass down, nigga!" I pointed the gun at him.

"I am your father and you pulling a gun on me!"

"Lower yo' tone, bitch! No father of mine would put me in the position you did, muthafucka! You ain't shit to me! Now answer the question!"

"I'm not telling you shit! You gon' do what the fuck you came to do anyway so, why the fuck should I tell you anything?"

"Yeah, that street nigga coming out. That's who I wanted to see. You couldn't put up the attorney façade any longer, huh?" I laughed.

"Laugh now, cry later. Yo' mama put her nose in my business and she came up missing, lil nigga."

"What you say?" I asked no longer laughing.

"I said yo' mama got in my business and left," he said trying to clean that shit up.

"Nah, that ain't what you said. Repeat that shit!"

"Since I'm gon' die anyway I might as well tell you the truth. Yo' mama threatened to go to the law about what I was into. I wasn't about to lose my career behind her jealous ass. She knew what the fuck I was into and was fine with it until she found out about Rodney Jr—"

"Rodney Jr? Nigga you only got one son," I growled.

"Yeah, it shows how much you know. Anyway, when she found out about him, she went into a jealous rage. She harassed his mother every chance she got and tried to fuck with my money and my freedom. I told her to worry about what I was doing for y'all but she wouldn't listen. When she threatened to go to the police, I made her disappear," he said cockily.

Hearing him say he did something to my mother brought tears to my eyes. I lowered the gun but never took my eyes off him. Rod didn't show any signs of remorse. For years I was told my mother left and didn't want me. To find out this nigga killed her hurt like hell. I just needed him to come out and say it.

"Who is this nigga that was the cause of my mother's demise?" I asked calmly.

"You know him very well," he laughed. "He's more street than you will ever be! I taught him everything about the drug game because he has the heart you never possessed. That's the reason I didn't want you out there. He knows all about you, but the difference between the two of you, he listens to me. I told him don't ever tell anyone that y'all are related."

"Who the fuck is he!" my voice boomed as I raised my Nina again.

"It's Shake, Pierre—"

"My muthafuckin' name is Psycho! That nigga used to grin in my face and he's been gunning for us for weeks!" I chuckled. "It's cool. Where is my mother, nigga? That's all I want to know."

He sighed long and cocked his head to the side. "That bitch is still living under the sea like the Little Mermaid at the bottom of Lake Michigan. Last time I saw her she was wearing cement blocks as stilettos," he grinned.

Pew! Pew!

Before I could change my mind, I shot his ass between the eyes and caught him in the neck. His body crashed into the glass coffee table and I wanted to spit on his ass but I wasn't trying to lead the police to my doorstep. Fuck that nigga, he was going to hell and I'll see him there when my time came.

I walked into the bathroom and grabbed a pair of rubber gloves that were sitting on the sink. As I was putting them on, I walked back into the living room and I heard Rod's phone chime. I searched through his pockets until I found it and he had a new text message from Floyd. Opening the message, rage filled me once again.

Floyd: Aye Rod, you got to get to Metrosouth Medical Center on 129th and Gregory Street in Blue Island. Shake was shot! Get here nigga!

Entering the information in my phone, I put Rod's phone in my pocket and made my way to the basement. I found a few cans of lighter fluid and went back upstairs. Covering the room with the liquid, I made sure I got Rod's body good and wet. I made a trail all the way to the bottom of the basement stairs and grabbed a towel from the cabinet.

Striking the lighter, I watched the flame grow on the towel and tossed it into the lighter fluid. The room lit up like a Christmas tree. I eased out of the door and walked through the alley, taking the long way to my car. I thought about my mother and I wanted to kill everybody that Rod was associated with. Starting with Shake. When I got to my car, I pulled out my phone and texted Ricio.

Psycho: where you at, my nigga?

I started the car and pulled out of the parking space. As I stopped at a stop sign, Ricio texted back.

Ricio: We still at my crib. You good?

Psycho: Nah, but I will be. I'll be there in a minute.

Making my way to the expressway, I headed to Ricio's crib with tears in my eyes.

Meesha

Chapter 4
Ricio

Seeing my brother being lowered in the ground was weighing heavy on my mind, not to mention the shit Nija said to me at the cemetery. I messed up with her but dwelling on it wasn't about to cloud my judgement. I had other shit to deal with and fighting with her wasn't one of them. We've been rocking too long and I knew for a fact, she'd be back.

After Beast jumped in my ride, I pulled off fast to follow Nija to the expressway. The grip I had on the steering wheel was deadly. At that point, I wished it was her fuckin' neck.

"Slow yo' ass down, Ricio!"

I didn't notice how fast I was going until Beast said something. My eyes were trained on the back of Nija's car. Easing my foot off the gas, I huffed loudly as I loosened my hold on the steering wheel. My hands were clammy so, I wiped them on my pants. Thinking back to the brief conversation I had with her, I shook my head.

"Do you know Nija had the nerve to tell me it was over between us? After all we've been through, she gon' leave a nigga on the day I buried my brother! When I need her ass the most!" The hurt and anger was wrapped into one big ass emotion and I was ready to lash out. I merged onto the highway and Beast started his pep talk.

"Ricio, you have to understand the shit you put her through. How long did you think she would stand by your side without a commitment? A blind man can see how much she loves you and you took it for granted. Once a woman feels that love ain't enough if it's not given in return, it's a wrap. You're either gon' have to allow her to move on, or prove you love her just as much as she loves you. That means letting the other women go and settling down with only her. Are you ready to do that?" Beast asked.

I had to think about what he said and honestly, being tied down to one woman wasn't something I wanted to do. But Nija knew that already. I'd never lied to her about anything. "Unc, I'm twenty-one, there's plenty of pussy out there waiting to be sampled. Especially Officer Smith's."

I don't love these hoes, man! But I love the shit out of Nija's ass. Nobody gets as much outta me as she does. Shit, she got keys to my crib and access to my fuckin' money! I pay her bills every month, what more do she want?"

"She wants you, Ricio! Even I know that material shit doesn't move Nija, she has her own money. In my opinion, what she's asking of you isn't too much. Y'all been rockin' since the first time you laid eyes on her, according to you. And been joined at the hip ever since. One thing I can say is this, Nija set herself up for allowing you to do whomever you wanted all these years."

"Where the fuck she going?" I said out loud. "I told her to come to my house and she's ignoring what I said to her,"

Watching Nija's car exited the expressway at 95th street was all I could do. I didn't realize she was getting off because I had turned my head briefly. Chasing her ass was going to have to wait, I had to get to my crib. Beast was laughing and I didn't see shit funny.

"What's funny, nigga!"

"Yo' ass! You just said you weren't ready to settle down but you sitting here clockin' the woman's moves expecting her to jump when you say so. That's not how this shit works, Youngin'. If you want to have a say in what goes on in her life, make her yours then you will have that right. Until then, you can't tell her shit and expect her to follow your rules. Let her live her life, Ricio. If it was meant to be, it will be."

The shit Beast was yapping about was falling on deaf ears. Nija was going to be my wife one day but she had to be patient and let me get to that point. I wasn't about to sit back while she let the next nigga get close. She was going to have a homicide on her conscious because that nigga wouldn't be breathing long if I found out about him.

Turning the radio on, I increased the volume because I was done listening to Beast trying to fix my fuckin' life like that bitch on that tv show. Some of the things he said was a hunnid but I was pushing it to the back burner. There were other things that needed my undivided attention.

As I exited the highway and cruised down the street to my crib, I bent the corner and I saw all my people posted up out front. If they weren't well dressed and looked professional, I'm quite sure the muthafuckas that lived in the building would've called the law on their asses. I pulled up and let my window down.

"Follow me to the back. Y'all shit will get towed if I let y'all park there," I said waiting for them to get in their cars.

Leading the way to the guest parking lot, I cut my engine and got out. Alejandro and my uncles got out of a Mercedes truck, three burly niggas got out of a black Range Rover, and two cocky muthafuckas got out of a white Lexus. In my mind I knew those were my cousins and I was glad to finally meet them.

"Buen, sobrino?" (You good, nephew?) Alejandro asked as I walked up the steps to unlock the door.

"Yeah, I'm as good as I can be under the circumstances," I responded holding the door open for them to pass through. "All I want to know is if you took care of that."

"We will talk about that when we get inside your place. That's something you don't' want to discuss in the open," Sabastián said pushing the button on the elevator.

The doors opened and I pushed my floor number and rested my head on the wall. I was drained but I wasn't sleepy, I was tired of everything we'd been through and what was still to come. Stepping off the elevator, we walked down the hall to my crib. As I placed the key into the lock, my uncle Julio asked, "Where is Sosa?"

"He was behind me when we got on the expressway but he took off without me. I thought he would've met me here. I'll call him once we get settled inside," I said pushing my door open.

My alarm didn't beep when I entered and I knew I'd set it when I left earlier. I immediately snatched my bitch off my hip and moved forward into the living room. My uncles and cousins were right behind me ready to light up some shit.

Cutting the corner with my tool in hand with my finger on the trigger, I sighed and put my gun down. Rodrigo was sitting on the couch with the remote in his hand and a smile on his face. I glanced at the tv to see what had him smiling so hard. His face was plastered on the screen and the news lady looked scared for her life. His smile turned sinister the longer he stared at the image.

"What the fuck are you doing, brah?" I asked walking over to where he sat.

He looked up and saw all of us with guns drawn and he chuckled. "What the fuck were y'all gon' do with that shit? Y'all supposed to come in this bitch gunnin' for whoever was in this muthafucka," he said doubling over with laughter. "Y'all look like a bunch of weak niggas! But hey, check this out," he said excitedly. Rodrigo pressed rewind on the remote and let the footage play.

"We are at Lincoln Cemetery where Maximo Vasquez is being laid to rest. Reports of shots fired were brought to our attention and we came right over. There are no signs of any violence but the family is still on the premises. Maximo was the son of the legendary Kingpin Maurice "Reese" Williams. Williams was killed four years ago to gun violence—" the reporter stopped speaking with wide eyes.

Rodrigo appeared on the screen and I knew there wasn't anything good about to happen. He looked between the news reporter and the camera man several times, making the reporter nervous. *"Is there a reason you're here speaking on my father at a private event? We didn't request the presence of Channel Nine. You reporting the wrong shit, Linda! How about you tell the people how there's nobody in custody for my brother's murder!*

Let's address the Chicago Police on the investigation that they haven't looked into since the day my brother was killed. Now you want to make news by talking about old shit that happened four years ago with my father! Everybody knows what happened to Reese Williams and wasn't shit done about that shit either. Those niggas are still roaming the streets just like whoever gunned my brother down.

All you muthafuckas are useless! But I would be the one getting twenty to life if I went out to do my own investigation. Get yo' ass away from here and go find another muthafucka to do a story on! And tell those fat muthafuckin' cops to lay off the doughnut shops and solve some of these damn murders around this city! Shit tell them to hire me, I'll find every one of them niggas."

The cameraman was running back to the van without turning the camera off. It was funny as hell but now wasn't the time to join in on Rodrigo's joy. Beast walked over and snatched Rodrigo up by his collar.

"What the fuck is yo' problem, Rodrigo? Do you know how much pressure you put on the cops that we have working for us? You just put a target on your fuckin' head dummy! The police gon' fuck with you just for the hell of it with that stunt you pulled!"

Beast, I respect you but get yo' muthafuckin' hands off me," he said yanking away from him. "I can do what the fuck I want to do. The police ain't out there trying to find out shit and that bitch was there trying to get a story by using my brother and father. Not on my muthafuckin' watch."

"Sosa—"

"Where that nigga at, Alejandro?" Rodrigo asked looking behind him then back at Alejandro. "Sosa is sleep! I'm Rodrigo and I would advise you to learn the difference between the two of us! I know you about to say something reasonable and I don't want to hear nothing you have to say. I'm going about this shit my way!"

Brah, you need to listen! That shit was reckless and you just brought heat our way. We can't go out and touch these niggas because they are about to be watching us now. We have to lay low," I said shooting daggers at his ass.

"Lay low if that's what ya'll want to do. That's a problem for you niggas, I move in silence! How the fuck you think half of their westside crew is jumping over fireballs in hell? Yeah, like I thought. Don't question anything I do. Y'all can sit back and make all these plans of running up on these muthafuckas.

I'm going about this shit without a plan because wherever the fuck I see them, it's lights out. I wasn't joking when I said I'd sit in a cell behind all of them." Beast walked up to Rodrigo and placed his hand on his shoulder. Rodrigo shrugged his hand off and took a step back. "You can say what you have to say without touching me,

Beast. I'm not the one for you to be trying to chastise because I'm a grown ass man just like you."

"I'm not going that route with you, nephew because I will fuck you up! All I want you to know is you have to calm yo' ass down. Ricio is correct, you messed up saying all that shit on live tv! We want revenge too, but you just put us all in a compromising position with the shit you said today," Beast tried to explain.

"I didn't put y'all in shit!" Rodrigo said as his phone started ringing. Snatching it from his hip, he looked at the screen and answered. "Yeah, Sin."

"What the fuck were you thinking?"

"Not you too!"

"The police are about to be on us like white on rice. Sit your ass down somewhere, you doing too much now."

"You are worse than your man, but I hear you. I'll leave the shit alone for now, but them bitch ass niggas bet not come for me because all bets will be off. Another thing, I'm still killing a nigga if I see them in the streets. I gotta go because I need to know what happened to the niggas that shot you. You do remember that don't you, Sin?"

"Rodrigo don't try to make me feel guilty about what I said. I want to get back at them just as bad as you, but there's a time to do that shit, right now ain't the time. Pipe down and be easy. I'll check on you later," she said hanging up.

He looked at all of us and put his phone on the coffee table. "That was Sin and y'all got it. I'll sit back and chill," he said smoothly. I knew he was lying though. "Did y'all get them niggas?"

"We chased down the car that left last and they got away," Nicholás said.

"The muthafuckas we were after got on the highway and took off. We lost them too," Javier chimed in.

I looked at Alejandro and was praying that he had some good news for us. He was looking at his sons and nephews with disgust after they said the muthafuckas got away. Sabastián stepped up and looked at all of my cousins.

"It's all good, we will get them soon," he said calmly.

"No, it's not all good! They weren't trained to fail!" Alejandro yelled. "They were trained to kill!"

"If we were able to get to them, they would be dead! We are in a country we know nothing about and you expect us to know the twist and turns of the roads! I jumped at the opportunity because they shot up my cousin's burial service!" Angel jumped in to confront his father. "You won't stand here and ridicule us for something that was out of our control. Fuck this shit!" he said walking out onto the balcony.

"Angel come back here!" Alejandro yelled but, Angel ignored him. Alejandro took a step in the direction Angel went and Julio grabbed him by the arm.

"Nah, leave him alone. Let him cool off." Alejandro walked to the kitchen and came back with a glass of Remy. He was fuming and kept looking at the balcony door before he sat down in one of the arm chairs.

"Hold on, let's get back on track here. Two cars got away, we got that. What about the black Impala? Was it one of the ones that got away?" I asked taking the conversation back to the subject at hand.

"No, that one didn't get away, they are all dead. We chased them down the street and shot at them. I rammed the back of the car and it sped up down the street. The passenger started shooting at us but of course his bullets were wild. They turned down a street and lost control of the car, hitting a light pole. I got out of the car and shot into the Impala and left them there to die," Alejandro said with pride.

"So, tell me this, do you know if they are actually dead?" Beast asked with his arms crossed over his chest.

"No one could survive that impact and the bullets I pumped inside the car. They are dead."

My phone chimed and I looked at it and Psycho had texted me.

Psycho: Where you at my nigga?

Me: We still at my crib. You good?

Psycho: Nah, but I will be. I'll be there in a minute.

The thought of Psycho killing Rod was on my mind heavily. That nigga had to go and I hope he took care of that. I tuned back in on the conversation that was going on around me.

"How is Sin?" Sebastián asked Beast.

"She's fine, I sent her home to rest up."

"Aye, that was Psycho," I said before they got deeper into their conversation. "He's on his way here but he didn't give any information about what went down with Rod. I'm going to check on Angel, give me a holla when he shows up."

Walking to the balcony door that Angel stormed out of, I paused before sliding the door. My cousin was standing with his back turned as he admired the beautiful waters of Lake Michigan. His shoulders moved up and down with every breath he took. The blunt he raised to his lips flared up for a good thirty seconds and I knew he was trying to calm down with the deep toke.

"You good, cuz?" I asked as I stepped out the door.

"Yeah, I'm straight," he said with a strong accent. "That muthafucka is gon' say the wrong shit one day and I'm going to knock his ass out. Nothing I do is ever good enough for him. He may be my father, but he will have to realize that I'm grown. It's time for him to let me live my life."

"Cuz, it's all good, don't let that shit bother you,"

"This didn't just start today, Ricio. The Vasquez family are control freaks, bullies, and pushovers. I'm tired of that shit, man. I'm twenty-three years old and I don't have no control of my life! He brought me to the wrong place, I'm never going back to the Dominican. I dealt with his bullshit long enough to make my own money, now I'm done," Angel said hitting the blunt.

"Angel I don't know what you've been through, but what I do know is that we're family. The one thing I will never do is turn my back on my own. You don't want to go back. You don't have to. Stay here with me and I got you cuz. Mi casa es su casa. (my house is your house) Tenemos mucho que ponernos al día," (We got a lot of catching up to do) I said smiling.

"I appreciate that, Ricio. Do me a favor though, don't speak Spanish to me no more. I hear enough of that shit back home."

"I can do that cuz. Welcome to America," I said dapping him up. "When are you going to tell Alejandro about your plans?"

"Fuck him," he laughed. "I don't have to tell him shit. I'm taking my life back and I will be the man I was destined to be without his ass."

"Angel, I think you should tell him what's on your mind. He can't make you do nothing, you're grown, right? What's the least he can do?"

"The only thing he's going to do is cut me out of his will," he hunched his shoulders and smiled. "Threaten me with money that I don't want. It don't mean nothing to me at all."

"I'm here for you, Angel. What I'm gon' do is go inside and bring Alejandro out here so y'all can talk it out," I said backing up toward the door. He didn't object so I opened the door and poked my head in, "Alejandro, come out here for a minute."

A couple minutes later, Alejandro appeared in the doorway with a glass in his hand. I guess he went back to my kitchen to get a refill of my Remy. Stepping out slowly, he glanced between me and Angel before speaking.

"What's going on?" he finally asked.

Clearing his throat, Angel stubbed out the blunt that he held in his hand and turned to his father. "What you did in there was put me on front street for the last time. I've done everything you've demanded of me my whole life. It stops today. See, I'm no longer the little boy that thought everything you said was law. I'm a grown man and it's time for you to realize that, you will not continue to control my life."

The eyebrow above Alejandro's left eye rose a notch. He bared his teeth like a Doberman pinscher ready to attack. Placing his glass on the table, he stepped in Angel's direction.

"Hear me loud and clear, son," he said calmly. "It's my job to make sure you do as I say. That shit was established when you exited my nut sack! You don't tell me what to say or when I can say it!"

Alejandro quickly collared Angel by his tailored shirt bringing them face to face. I took a step forward and my cousin reacted instantly, causing me to pause. "If you don't take yo' fuckin' hands off me, I'll act like I don't who the fuck you are!" Angel gritted his teeth and slapped his father's hand down.

"Eres malo ¿eh? Dime qué realmente piensas, Angel. (You bad, huh? Tell me what's really on your mind, Angel.)

"First of all, I want you to speak to me in English. Secondly, I'm tired of you treating me as if I'm still a kid, but want me to kill, sell illegal guns, and make money for you like a man. I can run your business in your absence and it still operates as if you hadn't left and I don't get any credit. I'm out, I'm not going back to the DR."

"What the fuck you mean? You have a job to do when we get home. You can't just quit. This is not up for debate!" Alejandro said loudly.

"You're right, there won't be a debate, I've already *told* you what's about to happen. I'm taking control of my life starting right now. Chicago is where I will be until I decide I want to go somewhere else, ain't shit you can do about my decision either," Angel shot back.

"There's something I can do about it alright. All I have to do is take your ass off my accounts and out of my will! You want to live in this country, let me see how you'll survive broke. Once I cut you off, there's no coming back! Do you understand me?"

Alejandro was pissed off but Angel wasn't moved by his father's tirade. The look on his face read, 'I don't give two fucks about you being mad.'

"It doesn't surprise me at all that you threw that bullshit at me, as if money is everything. New country, new life, I'll make due," Angel said removing his wallet from his back pocket. "Here's yo' shit, I don't need it. Thank you for showing me the way to being my own boss," he said holding the bank card out toward his father.

"Oh, you want to be cocky with this shit, right?" he snatched the card from Angel's hand. "I will fuck you up, mijo! Don't ever disrespect me, motherfucker!" Alejandro yelled.

Angel leaned back on the railing with a grin on his face without a care in the world. Alejandro lunged at him swinging his fist and connected with Angels jaw. The haymaker Angel delivered in return had a major impact and sent his father to the pavement on bended knee.

"Okay, that's enough," I said pinning Angel to the railing.

"I told you I'm not a child! You put yo' hands on me, I returned the favor. You're lucky you're my father because anybody else would've gotten the shit beat out of them. I decided to give you a sample of your own medicine!" Angel barked trying to get out of my grasp. The door opened and the Vasquez clan emerged with Beast, Rodrigo, and Psycho behind them.

"What's going on out here?" Sabastian asked glancing at Alejandro getting up from the balcony floor.

"¡Este carbon está muerto para mi! Ya no te llamaré hijo mio, Angle! Jodiste con la única persona que tenia la espalda!" (This fucker is dead to me! I will no longer call you my son, Angel! You fucked up with the only person that had your back!) Alejandro pointed at his son. "You want to stay here fine, don't call me when shit don't turn out how you expect." Angel didn't give him the satisfaction of a response. He attempted to walk around Sabastian and Alejandro grabbed him by the arm.

"Let him go, bro. He has a point. You brought this on yourself and we've had this discussion before. Respect is earned, not scared into anyone. This day has been coming for a very long time and I won't say, I told you so," Sabastian said pushing Alejandro back.

"Papí, we've talked about how you treat us as your sons, but it goes into one ear and out the other. Our opinions don't matter to you," Javier stated.

"I've seen this brewing for years and Angel has been saying he's sick of your shit for everyone to hear, uncle Alejandro. You just ignored it with the 'it's my way or no way' speech," Mateo said putting in his input. "If it wasn't for me, you and Angel would've bumped heads long before now."

"I raised you boys without mercy! Spoiling them was never my plan and I did what I had to do as far as discipline. Angel is one ungrateful son of a bitch and he's going to learn the hard way that nothing can be done without me!"

"Alejandro, I don't know you as a man, but listening to you talk about your son like he's a worker on your team, you're a piss poor father."

"Not today, Rodrigo," Beast said trying to stop him before he got started.

"Fuck that! I see why you were against Reese now. He was a better man than you on his worst day. If I was Angel, I would've shot yo' ass! Cuz will be good here because I'm gon' make sure of it."

"Stay the hell out of my business, Boy!" Alejandro glared at Rodrigo.

Rodrigo laughed and ran his tongue over his bottom lip. "I got yo' boy. Yo' business became mine when you tried to punk yo' son in my presence. My heart don't pump pussy for nan nigga, remember that. I'm not one of yo' sons, I don't have to respect yo' bitch ass."

"I'm out of here," Alejandro huffed. "Ricio I came here to help you with these fuckers that murdered Max, but I'll leave before I have to destroy a member of my family." He said heading toward the door.

"Are you referring to me, bitch?" Rodrigo asked. "We can take this shit outside and handle this like men. All this subliminal talking ain't my cup of tea. I'll be your stress reliever while whooping yo' ass."

"Chill with that shit, bro! Everything don't have to be about fighting, we're family," I said trying to calm Rodrigo down. "It's all good, Alejandro. We got shit covered, thanks for showing up."

I kept my eye on my brother to make sure he didn't pounce. Alejandro disappeared inside and left the rest of us outside on the balcony. Hugo was shaking his head standing off to the side and his jaw was clenching and unclenching a mile a minute. Julio walked over to him resting his hand on his shoulder. He said something to him that only he could hear and he nodded his head.

"Leaving isn't an option for me. I'm riding this out 'til the end. I don't care what we have to do, I'm in," Mateo said out loud.

"I'm with Mateo. We came here to help eliminate the problem and that's what we'll do. If leaving is what y'all gon' do, it's all good. Y'all old as hell and will stand out anyway," Nicholas grinned.

"I haven't said much but, I agree. We can't abort this mission until the end," Alexander piped in.

My cousins were standing up for what they believed in and didn't give a fuck what their fathers had to say about it. I was honored because they were going against the grain and finally stepping out to make their own decisions. Waiting for one of my uncles to reject their plans, I stood silently while nodding my head in appreciation.

"If this is what ya'll truly want to do, I won't try to stop you. All of you have been through far worse and can handle things with the help of your cousins," Hugo said. "Make them muthafuckers pay for the shit they put this family through. Javier, talk to your brother and try to change his mind about his decision."

"That's something I won't step into. Angel's mind has been made up for a while and I'm backing him with whatever he decides to do. Papí has to change his thought process if he wants his son back in his life. Until then, I'm staying out of it," Javier responded.

"Well we are going to head back to the DR so Alejandro can get all his frustrations out without getting his ass beat. If ya'll need us, just give one of us a call," Sabastian said dapping us up.

When the elder Vasquez guys left, I turned my attention to Psycho. He was looking down at his phone and must've felt my eyes on him. Putting the phone away, he stepped forward with rage in his eyes.

"I killed my father and I don't feel bad about it. His ass killed my mama," he said as a tear ran down his face. "Rod told me that he threw her in Lake Michigan with cement blocks on her feet. I've spent years believing she left us and this nigga killed her so she couldn't go to the police."

"Damn, fam, that's fucked up. please tell me his ass suffered," I said giving him a brotherly hug.

"After hearing him say he killed my mama, I just shot his ass between the eyes and sent the house up in flames. He also told me that I had a brother. Ya'll ain't gon' believe this shit," Psycho gritted swiping his hand down his face. "Shake is Rod's son because he would never be a brother of mine."

"Get the fuck outta here! How didn't you know?" Beast asked.

"I was raised as an only child. Rod said that he told Shake to never mention he was his son. It's cool though, Shake is at Metrosouth Medical Center. Floyd texted Rod's phone to let him know Shake was in the hospital. The last text I received on the phone before I tossed it on the side of the road said, he was fighting for his life."

The information Psycho delivered fucked me up in the head. Rod loved his wife when we were growing up and I couldn't believe he killed her over some street shit. Knowing Shake was one of the niggas my uncles caught made me smile. Big Jim's team was getting weaker by the day and I was ready to put a plan together to get at Shake while he was laid up.

"He won't be fighting for long but he's safe as of now," I said staring out into the lake.

Chapter 4
Latorra

I couldn't believe the bitch that approached Ricio and I, came to the exact prison that I worked at. The guy that came with her saved her from getting her ass whooped. It's been almost a week since the incident but I couldn't stop thinking about it. Ricio's brother's funeral was Friday and I couldn't attend because I was scheduled to work a sixteen-hour shift. Here it was Wednesday and I still hadn't heard from Ricio.

"Smith! You've been switched to handle visitations because Taylor called off. Make sure you keep your eyes and ears open," my supervisor informed me.

Visitations was my second favorite thing that I loved to do after front desk. The visits were funny as hell when an inmate had several females show up to see if they were being truthful to them. Making my way to my new post, it was almost nine o'clock so the show was about to begin.

As the doors opened and the visitors started entering the area, I noticed the guy from a couple days ago walk in. His eyes connected with mine and he had a sinister look in his as he walked by. I had never seen him before the other day and he kind of scared me. Putting my hand on my mace in case I needed to use it, the inmates entered.

"Big homie, over here!" the guy that had been watching me yelled.

"Keep your voice down please," I said doing my job.

The guy he referred to as Big homie turned in my direction with his top lip curled upward. I didn't care because he knew the rules just like I did. His snarl slowly disappeared the longer he stared at me and it made me uncomfortable because I didn't need any of these inmates trying to come for me on any level.

"Why is this nigga grilling me like he knows me?" I asked myself.

A female's high-pitched voice redirected my attention across the room and I headed right over. A young inmate by the name of

Thompson was trying to defuse an altercation between two females, one of which had a baby on her hip. The trio had everyone's attention with their drama and I wasn't in the mood for it.

"How the fuck you gon' have this bitch in here when you knew I was coming? You claim you ain't fuckin' wit her but she always finds her way back into your life."

Baby girl had on a pair of white skinny jeans that had her camel toe screaming to be freed, with a pink and white shirt that matched her pink Jordan sneakers. Her makeup was flawless and she was cute but, her weave was atrocious and looked like a bed of straw on her head.

"Aricka, calm that shit down, you gon' get my visit cancelled. I wanted both of ya'll here to talk about the baby. You knew this already because we talked about it last week."

"Nah, you talked about that shit! I told you I wasn't dealing with this bitch, period. You don't listen and you're always trying to force shit on me. What the fuck I look like being buddy buddy with a bitch you cheated on me with and made a whole fuckin' baby!" The other woman stood back watching the exchange between the two of them without uttering a word.

"You accepted that muthafuckin' ring after learning about my seed and you were down for whatever when I was on the street. Now you want to switch shit up as if all of this is one big surprise to you! All I want you to do is help her with my seed until I get out and you can't even do that."

"I don't have no kids, Earl! I'm not helping with shit that don't belong to me! Now make her leave because this is my day, nigga!" Aricka screamed.

"You don't have to worry, I'm leaving. Earl, I'll continue to send pictures of the baby but I won't be back," the baby mama said making her way to the exit.

"Sia—" Earl called out behind the woman.

"I'll beat yo' ass if you chase that bitch!" Aricka said with death in her eyes. Thompson paused staring at her evilly. He stepped toward Aricka with aggression.

"Okay, visit over, Thompson," I said putting a halt to his movements before he could touch Aricka. "You know disrupting visits aren't allowed and the consequences of what happens when it occurs. Come on, it's time to go back to the Block."

"Smith, let me stay. I promise to keep my voice down. I have to talk to her about my seed. See this is what's up—"

"That's for y'all to discuss on your own time, you're on mine now and I said the visit is over," I said cutting him off.

"I rode too far on that nasty ass bus to leave before my time is up. In other words, I ain't going nowhere!" Aricka said rolling her eyes. One of the other officers came over to assist in the matter before I could go off on her nappy headed ass.

"Oh, sweetie, the choice is not yours. How you got here is something you should've taken into consideration before you caused a scene. You'll have to wait the three hours sitting on the curb, but you getting out of here right now. Reed, take Thompson back to his cell."

"Hold up, Harvey! Do me a solid and let her stay, man," Thompson pleaded.

"Nah, if I let this slide, others will think it's cool to act the same way. The one you should've been begging for was ya shorty," Harvey said grabbing Aricka by the arm to escort her out.

"I know how to walk! You don't have to touch me!" she yelled snatching away."

"Aricka, I'm gon' call you tomorrow," Thompson yelled after her.

"Fuck you!" she said without looking back.

"The show is over people," I said walking back to my post. I noticed the guy that was yelling across the room earlier coming toward me and I sighed hard. He pulled out some money and inserted it into the vending machine next to me.

"Hello Miss lady," he said making his selection on the machine. "My brother wants to holla at you for a minute."

"I don't fraternize with the inmates on a personal level so, speaking with me won't be possible. I don't know him anyway," I responded without making eye contact. "Get your snacks and continue your visit." The mystery man took his chips and strolled back to the table and sat down.

Whispering something to the inmate, the burly dude turned his head glaring at me before he resumed his conversation. For the entire three hours it seemed I was the center of their conversation and I didn't like anything about it. Many officers took the bait of doing illegal shit for these prisoners, not me, I loved my freedom too much.

After the last inmate exited the visiting room three hours later, I went to the front of the prison to take my position behind the front desk. Before I could settle down to start the paperwork that was piled high, in walked my supervisor. By the look on his face, I knew whatever he was about to say wasn't going to be good for me.

"Smith, I need you on D Block. We are down an officer and you are the only one that can cover."

"Why can't you do it? I don't like the way the inmates gawk at me. That's the reason I was put at the desk the first week I started."

"I accommodated your wishes the best I could. When you were hired, flexibility was one of the first things that we talked about. You were trained to assist in any position as needed. Now, if you can't do the job, you can leave and don't return."

This muthafucka had his nerve and he was lucky I needed this job. "Fine, whatever," I said standing to my feet with an attitude. Snatching the walkie off the desk, I attached it to my shirt and stormed toward the door that led to the maximum section of the prison. I took my time getting to my destination and contemplated turning around and walking out. The bills that I knew would start piling up, flashed through my mind kept me moving forward.

The moment I stepped into the day room, the first person I saw was the dude that wanted to talk to me during his visit. He was sitting at a table playing cards and I was glad he didn't see me. One of the guys noticed me and made my presence known.

"Damn that CO is fine as fuck, my nigga! Where the hell she come from?"

All eyes landed on me and I felt naked standing in the doorway. Refusing to let them see me sweat, I put on a mean mug and started walking around making sure nothing was poppin' off. Chuck, another CO was on the far side of the room and I was glad because I wouldn't be able to handle anything alone.

"I don't know but that bitch is thick as fuck in that uniform. I'd bend that ass over and have a field day with her," one of the other dudes said.

"Cut that shit out and stop being so disrespectful! Show the lady some respect, lil nigga!"

"Damn Big Jim, let us have some fun around this muthafucka. It's not every day we see a fine bitch come through here."

"His name is Big Jim. I would have to look up his alias on the computer when I get back to my post," I said to myself.

"You heard what the fuck I said," Big Jim said getting to his feet. Heading straight for me, I became nervous with every step he took. "Don't pay them fools no attention. Nothing will happen to you as long as I'm around," he said when he approached me.

"I'm not worried about any of that. What can I help you with Big Jim?" I asked looking up at him.

The look of recognition was back in his eyes as he stared down at me and it made me uncomfortable so I stepped back a bit. He didn't respond right away but he never diverted his gaze away from me. Running his hand over the top of his head, he blinked a couple times before speaking.

"Are you from the Southside of Chicago?" he asked.

I was shocked he would ask me something so personal. I gave him a snide remark in return, "That's not your business."

"I only asked because you look familiar, that's all. You look like a woman named Rosalind that lived in the Englewood area."

When this man that I didn't know mentioned my mama, curiosity got the best of me. "What about her?" I wanted to know.

"You know her?" he asked.

"I know a lot of Rosalind's," I said trying to throw him off.

"She lived right off 71st and Ashland. Her mother's name was Betty and the last time I saw her she was pregnant. I searched high and low for that woman but I couldn't find her. Betty didn't want her to be with me because of what I did to make money but, there was nothing that could stop the love we had for each other. At least that's what I thought. Rosalind must've been forced to get rid of the baby because there was no way she would've kept me away from my child."

Hearing Big Jim talk about members of my family that were no longer on earth, had tears running down my cheeks. I remembered my grandma saying that my father was a good for nothing street thug but I didn't know what it meant as a child. But I knew the man standing before me couldn't be him.

"You alright, baby girl?" he asked with concern in his voice. "You know the people I mentioned, don't you?"

Wiping the tears from my face, I shook my head up and down. I didn't want to discuss anything with this man but, he seemed to have known my mama before the drugs became the focal point of her life. It's been a while since I've heard anything nice about my mama since her passing seven years prior.

"She was my mama and Betty was my grandma," I said lowly.

Big Jim reared his head back with a shocked expression on his face. "What do you mean *was*?" he asked.

"Grandma Betty passed away when I was twelve years old and my mama and her boyfriend was murdered two years later. I've been on my own since I was sixteen and my life is now starting to look bright again. I don't want to talk about this anymore, go back to the table with your friends," I said taking a step away from him.

"Did Rosalind have any kids before you?"

Turning back around to face him, I scowled at him because I had just said I didn't want to talk anymore. "No, I was her only child. Would you leave me alone and drop the subject, please? I just want to get through this work day and go home. You know my family, great. But don't think you will get to know me," I said walking off.

Chapter 5
Big Jim

When Floyd came to visit me, he said he had something to discuss with me. I stepped into the room and this fool hollered out like we were on the street. A female officer that I'd never seen before checked his ass nicely and he piped the fuck down. When I got to the table, he started talking right away.

"What up, Big? I tried to come see you on Tuesday but when I got here, the chick I had with me got into an altercation with the CO over there," he said nodding toward the cutie in uniform.

"Why the fuck would you bring somebody that's not even on my list with you, nigga?" I asked seriously. "And why didn't you come back the next damn day?"

"She had some information about Ricio for me and I needed to hear her out. Coming back was something I couldn't do. We spent most of the day looking for Red until I got a call informing me that Ricio and his crew was hitting the spots."

"And you didn't think to call me to tell me what was going on? I went to the wake to make sure Max's ass was truly dead and got the surprise of my life, nigga. Red is dead, Floyd. They did him dirty as fuck and I didn't get a heads up that he was even missing. You fucking up in these streets. What else is going on out there that I should know about but don't?"

"I sent a crew to shoot up Max's burial, things didn't go as planned." Floyd said.

"What the fuck you mean it didn't go according to plan? Somebody died right?"

"Yeah, three of our men. Rell, Boogie, and Tez. Shake is fighting for his life at Metrosouth."

"What the fuck, nigga! I have never known you to botched up so much shit, Floyd! I gotta get the fuck outta here before my whole muthafuckin' empire goes to shit because yo' ass is scared of some young niggas. You supposed to be out there going to war with everybody else, but all I've heard is you sending muthafuckas on blank missions. What have you been doing all this time?"

"I've been conjuring up a plan with the information that I got from the chick I was trying to tell you about. She is the sister of a bitch Ricio fucks with," he said as he stared behind me. "The female CO is fucking with that nigga too. I found that out when shawty was trying to get at her last week."

I turned to see who he was talking about and baby girl looked familiar as hell. "Go over there and tell her to come holla at me," I said turning back around. Floyd was gone for less than two minutes before he was back with a bag of chips. "What happened? I don't see her moving."

"She said she won't be coming over here because she don't interact with the inmates."

Glaring at the CO that refused to talk me, I turned my attention back to Floyd. He may be my right-hand man, but he was on his way out of my camp if he didn't make something happen soon. "What else do you got that will help us get closer to Ricio?"

"I know where the sister works and where she lives. I haven't seen any movement on her crib so she has to be laying low somewhere else. She will be getting a visit at her job tomorrow, I'm gon' handle that myself. I also have an address on her best friend and I have a couple of the lil niggas going by there this evening."

"Stay on top of that shit and leave the CO to me. I will have her on our side in no time. Don't leave me out of the loop about shit else! I want to know when yo' ass take a shit before you wipe yo' ass! This is your last shot, no more fuck ups or it's lights out for you, nigga. Check on Shake and I want an update asap.

In the meantime, I'm gon' holla at Rod to see what he can do to get me out of this bitch. It's a good thing they don't know he's on my payroll. He would have to watch his back too if that was the case. Hold shit down the way I've taught you and shit should be good. I'll be out in a minute, nigga. We gon' end this once and for all," I said standing up out of my seat and walking away without another word.

I went back to my cell and all I could think about was how I was going to get Officer Smith to cooperate and work for me. Finding out how deep she was into Ricio was something I needed to know and also if her hardcore demeanor could be broken. I would hate to have to strong arm her to do as I say, but I would.

My mind went back to the conversation the two of us had briefly and Rosalind's face appeared in front of me. Officer Smith was a spitting image of her mother which made me start counting back the years in my head. She was about twenty-three if my calculations were correct. At some point I fell asleep and I turned over onto my back. My movements alerted my cellmate that I was awake and he thought that meant he could start talking.

"Aye, Big Jim. Can I get a pack of your noodles until I get my commissary?" my cellmate asked breaking my thoughts.

"Nigga, it's about to be chow time! You can wait fifteen minutes to eat the nasty shit that's provided in this bitch. My shit is not part of a food pantry," I said getting up to take care of my hygiene.

"Is that a no?"

Ignoring his ass, I went to the sink and started brushing my teeth with the flimsy ass toothbrush we were forced to use. The sound of muthafuckas roaming around let me know it was time for me to leave the cell before I killed this nigga.

Walking to the door, I turned around and eyeballed my cellie. "Don't touch shit, if anything is missing you will be spending the night in the infirmary."

As I walked into the hall, I spotted Officer Smith turning the corner. Working out was my plan but when I laid eyes on her, those plans went out the window. She tried to walk past me but I wasn't about to let that happen.

"Good morning, Officer Smith." She ignored me and tried to keep walking. I gently grabbed her arm and she looked down at my hand. Letting her go, she took a step, "I'm your father," I said before she could waltz away.

Her feet stopped instantly like she was programmed to halt. She turned to face me and her eyes had a look of wanting in them but only for a millisecond. "How the fuck you think you're my father? Oh, because you know of my mother and granny? That don't mean shit, Carter." She seethed.

"Let me explain," I said pausing to make sure she didn't cut me off. "I was with your mother for years. She was the love of my life. Your grandmother didn't agree with Rosalind being with me because I was a street nigga. Our relationship was forbidden in her eyes and she did everything to keep us apart.

When your mother told me she was pregnant, I was the happiest man on earth. But I couldn't say the same about Betty. Rosalind would sneak around to see me after school so her mother wouldn't find out. I made sure she was straight by giving her money to take care of herself. Betty wanted her to get rid of the baby but your mother fought tooth and nail to keep it.

We talked about moving her out of her mother's house but it never happened. One day I waited for Rosalind to show up at my crib but she never came. When I went to the house, it was empty. Betty had moved her away and turned her phone off. Looking high and low for Rosalind, they couldn't be found." I explained.

"What is this supposed to mean to me? I'm twenty-three years old and I've never had a father. My life was shitty when my mother was killed and here you are talking about you my daddy. You have only been locked up a short time, if what you said is true, why didn't you try harder to find her? Her murder was in all the newspapers and all over the news but you had no clue she was dead."

Stop trying to blow smoke up my ass and tell me what you really want with me? If not, stay your ass away from me. I don't have time for bullshit, Carter. Knowing you, the man that was here to see you yesterday gathered enough information on me so you could make up that sad as story." She sneered.

"I wouldn't make something like this up. Hearing you say that Rosalind was your mother had a nigga thinking about the shit all night. You are an only child and your age is on point. There's no way you're not my daughter, Smith. I have a sister named Lynetta that lives on 83rd and Muskegon.

Stay right here for a minute, please," I said backing up into my cell. Hurriedly scribbling the information on a piece of paper, I returned to the hall. "Please give her a call, she can vouch for everything I've told you today. I will even set up an appointment to get a

52

DNA test done and if you're not my daughter, I won't say anything else to you."

She looked at the paper and folded it up putting it in her pocket. Officer Smith shook her head and walked away. I didn't know if she was going to use the information or not, I would have to wait and see. I watched her stroll slowly through the corridor with her shoulders slightly slumped until she turned the corner.

Entering my cell, I dropped to the floor and started doing pushups. The count in my head reached fifty before I started good. My arm and core muscles were burning but I kept going. After doing another one hundred pushups, I eased up and started running in place which led to short sprints. The frustrations I was feeling made me give my body an extreme workout.

Rosalind's face appeared before me and I shook the image away. Lying on my back I started doing crunches like my life depended on it. the sweat dripped in my eyes but I didn't let up. Floyd's fuck ups came to the forefront of my mind and I pushed harder. He'd always been on his shit until recently. Something was going on with him and I was determined to find out what his issue was.

My empire was at stake and I refused to let him take it down with him. Thirty minutes later I was done but the frustrations were still there. Grabbing a towel, I rushed to the showers to freshen up. When I walked in, there was a young nigga pulling a shirt over his head. His face was revealed and I recognized him as one of the new prisoners that came in a week prior.

He was getting his ass whooped from day one until I stepped in to protect him. For a price of course. "What's up Big Jim?" he spoke.

Nodding my head, I walked to an empty stall and turned the nozzle. I stepped under the stream of water and let it cascade down my back. The tension in my body didn't ease up because the showers in the prison wasn't shit like I remembered out on the street.

"Aye, come suck my dick, nigga!" I barked at the young nigga.

Sexual favors were his way of paying me to keep them muthafuckas off his ass. He became my low-key stress reliever and never complained. He entered the stall dropping to his knees and gulped my joint into his mouth with no hands. The way his jaws locked on my shit had my toes curling. My head fell back against the wall and my stomach tightened.

Shooting my load down his throat, I stepped under the water and turned my back on him. "Get the fuck out," I barked with my eyes closed. There was so much that needed to be done and I couldn't do shit because I was locked away in a hell hole.

Chapter 6
Nija

I jumped out my car with briefcase in hand because I was running late for work. When I stepped inside the building, it was filled to capacity. Many didn't look too happy that they would have to wait and it was a clear sign the day would be shitty even though it had just begun. Walking down the hall to my office, one of my coworkers stopped me before I entered.

"Girl, these folks ain't playing. Tangie and Miriam have already gotten cursed out. I want one of these little bitches to come at me sideways, I'll be fired after dragging her ass."

"I'm waiting on the day somebody disrespects me. I just buried my brother and I got steam to let loose. Let me get in here and get my caffeine fix. Don't let these people get to you," I laughed as I entered my office.

The first thing I did was put a mocha Frappuccino in my Keurig and powered on my computer. I opened my briefcase and took out the files I'd taken home to look over. I had so many appointments lined up that I was overwhelmed just by looking at them. Grabbing the mug from the machine, I took a sip and closed my eyes. That one sip gave me life.

When the computer finally booted up, I was ready to work. My first appointment was at nine o'clock so it gave me fifteen minutes to get situated. As I was going through one of my files the phone rang. Not bothering to look at the display, I snatched the receiver off the base.

"DHS this is Nija speaking, how may I help you?"

"Ni, why am I still on the block list? Get me off that shit, man!" Ricio's voice boomed in my ear.

"What did you do, wake up and watch the clock until you knew I'd be at work?"

"Actually, I did. I've been trying to call and I keep getting your voicemail. I figured after a couple days, it'd give you time to think about shit but, you still avoiding a nigga! We are forever and I'm not trying to hear that shit you talking about. Ain't no breaking up!"

His ass sounded dumb as fuck. How were we breaking up when we were never together? This was how niggas acted when they knew it was a possibility another man could play the position they took for granted.

"Ricio, I'm at work and I don't have time to talk about this—"

"You ain't had time in six muthafuckin' days, Nija!"

"Lower your voice when you're talking to me, Mauricio. We discussed this at the cemetery and I said what I said, I'm done. Wasn't I there to get you through one of the worse days of your life? I held up my end of the bargain, now leave me the fuck alone," I said low and stern before slamming the phone down.

How dare his ass call me so early with his bullshit. Ricio had me fuming and it only took five minutes to take me from zero to sixty. Letting him get to me was something I wasn't about to do. The ringing of the phone irritated me even more because I knew it was him once again.

"What!" I said without saying hello.

"Nija, hear me out. There's too much going on for me not to be able to contact you. Just take me off the list."

"I'll take you off, but the minute you call and you're not making sure I'm breathing, I'm blocking your ass again. What we had is over. Go harass one of the many hoes you be parading around the city with."

"What have I told you about worrying about other muthafuckas? They don't mean shit to me! You the one that has access to everything I own, including my heart. I pay yo' bills, you ain't never gon' want for shit! Concentrate on what we got, nothing else should matter."

"You of all people should know, material things don't mean nothing to me! Throw your money in the faces of those needy hoes that can't or should I say, won't hold a fuckin' job. The ones that's looking for a nigga like you to take care of their ass. As a matter of fact, don't pay shit else for me! I've told you long ago I was capable of taking care of myself financially."

All I wanted you to do for me was show me the same love I've shown you for years. It doesn't pay to be the loyal bitch to you niggas. Being there in every way imaginable, professing love, putting my life on hold, and for what? Just so the muthafucka can continue to shit on you and expect you to accept what he's doing. Nigga, please."

I know my worth, Ricio! I'm gonna say this for the last time, I refuse to be second to any bitch! I'll stand alone before I lower my standards for anybody! I've sat back and waited too long with no results. It didn't matter what I did, you were still blind to the shit. Now, I have work to do. Have a nice day."

Tears streamed down my face as I placed the phone on the cradle. I was too good of a woman to waste my time on a man that wasn't ready for commitment. I've invested too much time into Mauricio and I wasn't going to spend another minute waiting for him to figure his shit out. My life was valuable and it was time for me to live. I'm too young to sit back watching my life pass by.

I've loved him from the day he showed me what love was. He couldn't possibly love me the way he claimed because if he did, my heart wouldn't hurt behind his stupidity. I couldn't make him be with me, but my life would go on.

Glancing at the clock on the wall, I had three minutes to go out and get my first client. After dropping Visine in my eyes, I touched up my makeup, snatched the file off my desk and left my office. I had to force the conversation with Ricio out of my mind in order to conduct business professionally.

"Shonda Rhymes," I called out when I entered the lobby.

"Right here," a tiny voice replied. Shonda was struggling to balance an infant and her belongings at the same time. Feeling sorry for her, I walked over and took the bag from her hand. "Thank you."

"No problem, follow me," I said leading the way to my office.

Once we were seated, I looked at her file and she had applied for benefits when she was pregnant and was only awarded medical coverage. "I have a couple questions for you Shonda. Answer them truthfully and I will do my best to help you any way I can, okay?" she nodded her head and I continued. "Are you working right now?" I asked.

"Shonda took a deep a deep breath shaking her head no. "I was working but when I went into labor, I didn't show up for my shift and they fired me. The manager denied my unemployment stating I was always late and didn't show up for my shift. It was a lie but I couldn't prove any of it because she had changed my time in the system to match her story. Come to find out, she's messing with my daughter's father."

Listening to her tell her story only pissed me off but I had to mask my feelings because I wasn't her friend. That's the one thing I wasn't about to be in the street, a bitch wandering around looking stupid while in love. The nigga was fucking around right under her nose and didn't care how that would've affected her.

"Do you live alone or have anyone that helps you with living expenses?" I asked when I gathered my thoughts.

"No, it's just me and my baby. My section eight came through a couple months before I went into labor. My rent is zero at the moment because I don't have a job. But I don't have money for food and milk for my baby," she explained. "Y'all can keep the cash because when I hit her father with child support, I want every dime that she's entitled to."

I liked the way she thought things out. A lot of these young girls were only worried about themselves. This young lady was thinking about her baby from what I was hearing. It made me want to help her even more.

"What is your daughter's father's name and social security number?"

"Miss Nija, I'm gonna give you the information you're seeking, but I don't want his name on any of my paperwork," she said digging in the side pocket of the diaper bag. "Here is the documentation from the child support office," she said passing them to me. "He's going to help me take care of this baby if he wants to or not. I don't want to be here but I don't have a choice. My baby is my first priority and I'll do whatever it takes to make sure she's good."

Typing away on the keyboard after scanning the papers she gave me I was satisfied with the results I came up with. Adding her to my list of clients, I printing out a couple pages she would have to sign, I turned my attention back to Shonda. Handing the child support papers back to her, I sat up straight in my chair.

"Okay, Miss Rhymes, I've approved you for three hundred fifty-dollars' worth of food stamps. It will be available on your EBT card the fourth of each month."

"That's two weeks away!" she exclaimed.

"Shonda, let me finish what I'm saying before you jump to conclusions. You will leave here today with one hundred seventy-five dollars applied to your card. Your medical benefits will be the same as its been and I've made an appointment for you at the Women Infant and Children office. That will help you with milk for the baby."

"Thank you so much," she cried hugging her baby. "I'm grateful for your help. Being a mother at nineteen, learning everything alone is hard."

"You're welcome. Here is my card, call me if you have any questions. Make sure you contact me whenever you start working. Do not try to bypass calling because the minute you start punching a clock, it will appear in the system," I explained pushing the papers toward her to sign. "Sign here, here, and here. You will be contacted by mail when it's time to recertify."

Shonda finished signing the papers and that concluded our time together. I stood and shook her hand before I escorted her to another area to get her EBT card. Returning to my office, I looked at the next file and went out to grab the next client.

I was busy nonstop and I almost worked through lunch. When I finished up with the woman that gave me a very hard time, I stared at the clock and noticed it was one thirty and I was starving. I snatched my purse out of my drawer and headed out the door to get something to eat.

Deciding to walk to the barbeque joint up the street, I heading south on Cottage Grove. Half a block into my walk, I heard someone behind me and I turned around but there was no one there. Something in my mind was telling me to go back to get in my car but I kept going. Five minutes later I was in line to order my food when a guy came in and stood directly behind me. He was so close that I could feel his breath on the back of my neck.

"Excuse me, but can you please step back off me, please?" I asked nicely.

"Oh, my bad, shawty. I didn't mean to alarm you. I've never eaten here, is it any good?"

"Yeah, their food is pretty good," I said walking to the counter to place my order.

"What can I get you today, hun?" the lady behind the glass asked.

"I would like a large turkey tip with extra barbeque sauce and an extra slice of bread please."

"Okay, that will be ten fifty," she said.

Putting my card through the slot, I waited while she ran my card while looking around the restaurant. The guy that was behind me must've changed his mind about eating there because he was gone. Not thinking anything of it, I stepped aside after getting my card and receipt and waited for my number to be called.

It didn't take long for my food and I was out in less than fifteen minutes. The aroma that traveled from the bag had my stomach doing a happy dance and I couldn't wait to sit down to savor the taste. Hurrying out the restaurant, I walked briskly down the street. Once again, I heard footsteps behind me but no one was there when I turned around.

I was glad I decided to wear flats because I picked up my pace damn near running back to my job. When I got inside the building, Tangie met me in the middle of the room like she had some good tea to spill. She was going to have to hold that thought because I was hungry as hell and I needed to eat before I could even attempt to get back to work.

"What's going on?" I asked trying to walk to my office.

"I wanted to let you know, your sister is in your office waiting for you," Tangie said.

"My sister? What's her name?" I asked as I stopped walking.

"When I asked, she said you only had one sister and refused to tell me."

"Don't let nobody in my personal space. I don't care if they say they're my mama, make them wait out here with everybody else," I said storming off.

The last thing I wanted to do was deal with Nihiyah and her bullshit. Especially at my place of employment. When I got to my office, Nihiyah was sitting behind my desk like she was getting paid instead of me.

"Nihiyah what are you doing here?" I asked closing the door.

"Hello to you too, baby sister. I wanted to stop in to see how you've been since I haven't talked to you since that day at the house."

Nihiyah looked like she hadn't slept in days and her hair was unkempt along with the clothes she wore. There was no way she could deny being on drugs because she looked bad. My mama couldn't have seen her because she would've called me in tears after doing so.

"Hiyah, what the fuck is going on with you?" I asked walking behind my desk. "Get out my seat and sit over there," I pointed to the chair on the other side.

"Ain't shit going on with me. I wanted to see my sister so I jumped up and came over here."

"You look like you haven't had a bath in days and your breath smell like a pile of shit. How the fuck you outside like this?" I was mad as fuck because she was at my job saying she was my sister, looking like a muthafuckin' crackhead.

"I need a few dollars so I can do laundry and get something to eat."

"Do I look stupid to you, Nihiyah? You live in a house that has a washer and a dryer with plenty of food in the fridge. What are you really trying to do because the shit you just said ain't it?" I asked opening the bag that held my food.

"I just told you what I needed to do—"

"And that's a fuckin' lie! Here, eat some on these turkey tips," I said placing a couple on a napkin.

"Nija, I didn't ask you for none of your food, I need some money," she yelled.

"Who the fuck you hollering at? A nigga that's hungry gon' take whatever is offered without complaints. Right now, you sound like the junkies I despise out here in these streets. You hungry but won't take what's being given. I'm not going to sugarcoat shit. I'm not giving you any money."

"Why not? I told you I need that money."

"Nihiyah, you need to get your mind right. I won't enable you by givin' you money to put shit up your nose. Mama didn't raise us like that and you know it. I've given you the opportunity to tell me what you're going through and you've been dancing around the situation. Looking at you sitting before me today, you have a fuckin' problem."

"Fuck you! Your life ain't squeaky clean, bitch! For your information, I don't have a drug problem. My problem is, yo' ass helps everybody but your family!"

"Must I remind you again that I'm at work? Lower your muthafuckin' voice before I have you escorted out of here. It's bad enough I'm spending my lunch break sitting here constantly telling you no like you're a toddler. I don't have time to listen to you lie to my face another second. You are free to leave," I told her putting one of the turkey tips in my mouth.

"Don't dismiss me like I'm one of these muthafuckas you helping in this bitch! I'm your sister, Nija!" she screamed directly in my face.

I bent toward the garbage and threw up the food I was chewing. The smell that hit my nose smelled like she dumped an entire bowl of shit water in my face. Vomit spewed from my mouth and nose making it hard for me to breath. I was throwing up the lining of my stomach because wasn't shit in there besides the piece of tip and a half cup of Frappuccino.

After wiping my mouth with a napkin, I looked up at Nihiyah with fire in my eyes. "Get the fuck out, funky bitch! Go sit your ass in the lobby and get some assistance since you won't get off your ass to get a job!"

"I'm not going nowhere until you give me what I came here for!"

"Oh, you ain't gotta go home but you getting out of here!" I yelled picking up the phone. Before I could dial for security, my door opened and my boss walked in.

"Nija, is everything alright?" she asked. "I could hear ya'll all the way in my office. This is unacceptable."

"I apologize, Vera. Get Larry to escort this woman out of my office, please."

"It's against company policy for you to carry on with a client in this manner, Nija. I'm going to have to document this incident immediately."

"I'm on lunch, so that would mean there wouldn't be any clients in my office, Vera. This is my dumb ass sister and she's leaving. I'm not about to get reprimanded for something that's not associated with this job. Now, if you want to write me up for carrying on for others to hear, that's fine. But what you won't do is try to make it seem like I'm disrespecting clients," I said pushing the button for security on the phone.

"Larry, come to my office immediately please," I said hanging up. "Nihiyah, you will not disrupt my job with your bullshit. Don't ever come here again. I will never have a dime to give you and I'd advise you to seek help. You may be my sister, but I'll beat your ass like a bitch in the street."

Larry appeared in the doorway and I pointed at my sister with hurt in my eyes. "Get her out of here! She is not allowed back into this building until I give the okay."

"Fuck you, Nija. You gon' regret treating me like I'm not shit!" Nihiyah screamed as Larry grabbed her by the arm.

"No, I won't. Stop throwing idle threats, I'm not worried, Hiyah."

The movement of her mouth let me know that I was about to whoop her ass. She hocked up a mouthful of saliva and spit it toward me and it landed right in the middle of my food. I rushed around the desk and lunged for her ass. Vera stopped me by grabbing me around the waist while Larry dragged my sister out by the arm.

All the nosey muthafuckas were crowded around my office door taking everything in. I was so embarrassed because part of my life was on display for all to see. Vera released me and turned to the doorway.

"Okay, the show is over. Get back to work, there's nothing else to see!" she barked. "Nija, I've never had a problem out of you since you've been working here. If this happens again you will be in the unemployment line. This is a place of business not a meeting spot for your family issues.

Take the rest of the day to get your mind together and I'll see you on Monday," Vera said stepping out the door.

"Monday? Today is Thursday, I do work on Fridays you know."

"Not this Friday you won't. Handle the problem with your sister and enjoy your weekend."

"What about the rest of my appointments? Who's going to take care of them?" I asked snidely.

"I'm going to take care of your caseload myself. Go home, Nija while you still have a job. Don't push me because I'm two seconds from firing you," she said leaving me standing in the middle of my office looking stupid.

I was pissed because my crackhead ass sister almost made me lose my fucking job. It was time for me to have a heart to heart with my mother and let her know just how deep her daughter was out here with a drug problem.

Chapter 7
Rodrigo

It's been a week since my little brother was laid to rest and I was sitting in my living room trying to find something to watch on the muthafuckin' tv. What I said to the reporter on live tv was the truth, I didn't see shit wrong with it. They should've minded their own business and stayed the fuck out of mine. That's what was wrong with the media, they wanted to water down the story and make it into something it wasn't. So, I gave the people the real deal.

Not giving a fuck about none of that, my main concern was killing a muthafucka. But with Ricio and Beast breathing down my neck, I couldn't scratch my nuts without being asked what I was doing. It was blowing the fuck out of me. My phone rang and my eyes instantly went to the screen. Nija's named appeared and I didn't hesitate to answer.

"What up, sis?"

"Sosa—"

"Sorry, Sosa is not available right now, but when the nigga come back to the surface, I'll tell him to call you," I said seriously.

"Rodrigo, this is not the time to play with me. One half of yo' ass *is* Sosa!" she cried out.

"Nija, what's wrong?"

"Where you at?" she asked in a panicky voice.

"At the crib, where you at?" I asked sitting up.

"I'm heading southbound on the Dan Ryan. I was on my way to my mama's house but there's a car following me and I don't want to lead whoever it is over there."

"Where are you exactly?"

"I'm passing 95th about to merge onto I57."

I could tell she was scared and I was about to get my chance to blow a muthafucka's wig back. I jumped up, grabbing my .357 mag and tucked it in the back of my pants as I headed for the door. "This is what I want you to do. Get in the slow lane and take your time on the expressway. I don't give a fuck who honks at you, keep going the speed limit." I said as I jumped in my whip. "That will give me time to get to you. What color is the car?" I asked backing out of my driveway.

"It's silver. Whoever it is has been following me since I pulled away from my job."

"Why are you off so early, Nija?"

"I got suspended but we can talk about that later. Where you at?"

"I just jumped on the e-way, what's your location?"

"I'm passing 127th. Bro, I'm scared.

"Okay, I'll meet you at the forest preserve on 147th. The one we had the barbeque at a couple years ago, do you remember?"

"Yeah, I know which one you're talking about. Which entrance?"

"Go in on Loomis and I'll be there waiting, I promise, sis. Are they still following you?"

"Yeah, right behind me. There's only one person in the car, bro," she said.

"That's even better. I'm still on the phone but let me know if anything changes in his movements. So far, it seems he is just trying to see where you going. But he's about to go to hell." I said as I turned into the preserve. Making sure the park was clear, I got out while screwing the silencer on my piece. "Where you at, Nija?"

"I'm coming down 147th and yes, he's still behind me."

"Good, lead his ass to me. I'm already here."

"How did you get there so fast?" she asked.

"Don't worry about that, I'm here and that's all that matters. When you pull in, I'll see you. Park beside my car, get out and run to the passenger side of my shit. you will be safe until I get rid of this nigga."

"I'm pulling in now."

"I see you and this fuck nigga. Keep coming and do what I told you to do."

How stupid could a muthafucka be to follow somebody without being conspicuous about it? I asked myself as I watched Nija pull up beside my car from the dumpster I was hiding behind. When her car door opened, the nigga jumped out of his ride and ran toward her. She had just enough time to close and lock the door before he could grab her.

"Get the fuck out the car, bitch! You about to pay for my brother getting killed since I can't find yo' man!" the nigga said pulling his gun from his waist.

He stepped back and fired twice at the window. Nija ducked down but neither one of them knew he wouldn't hit her because my shit was bulletproof. I crept up behind him with my tool in hand as he beat on the window trying to get in.

"Don't move muthafucka!" I sneered pushing the nozzle deep into the back of his head. The gun he held, fell from his hand and he tried to turn around. "If you move, I'm gon' blow yo' fuckin' head off! Who sent you, nigga?"

"This ain't got shit to do with you, man. I just want to talk to my bitch." Hitting him with the butt of my gun, he fell to one knee. I kicked his ass onto his back and when he saw my face, his eyes looked like they would pop out of the sockets. "Sosa—"

"Nah, playa, wrong muthafucka! Who the fuck sent you?" I barked slowly aiming at his head.

"Ricio killed my—"

"Ricio ain't did shit, bitch!" I said sending a bullet through his arm. "That bullshit right there let me know that Floyd sent yo' ass after my people. What else is he up to, nigga?"

"Aaaaaaarrrrrghhh!" he screamed rolling onto his side. I kicked him back onto his back and stepped on the arm I had just shot him in. The nigga was squealing like a pig and I loved it.

"What is Floyd's plan?" I asked again.

"Ain't no plan! They are making sure Shake gon' be good."

"If it ain't no plan, how the fuck you end up following my sister? You know, the one you called yo' bitch," I sneered.

"I—I—"

"I, I, my ass muthafucka, talk! Stop acting like you got a speech impediment all of a sudden. What the fuck was you sent to do?"

"I was told to follow her from her job and scoop her up. But I missed the opportunity when she went out for lunch because there were too many people out. I figured I'd follow her home and get her then."

"Okay, tell me this, how did you know where she worked?"

"Some crackhead bitch told Floyd where she worked, lived, and that she's the key to Ricio. I wanted the job because my brother was one of the niggas y'all killed last week!"

I laughed because he really thought I cared about that pussy ass shit. "Nigga, do it look like I give a fuck about yo' brother getting killed? If he's dead, that means he was with the muthafuckas that disrespected my brother that was being buried. Not to mention, the nigga that sent yo' stupid ass off is the one that killed him! I'm tired of listening to yo' idiotic ass, tell yo' brother I'll see him in hell."

Pulling the trigger repeatedly, I shot his ass in every part of his body. I reloaded three times and he was unrecognizable when I finished with his ass. Tapping on the window of my ride, Nija opened the door. Tears were rolling down her face and I kneeled down to look into her eyes.

"I need you to get into the driver seat and drive this muthafucka to my house," I said handing her the keys. Don't make any stops, go straight to my crib and text me when you get there. Calm yo' ass down before you pull off. Tear my shit up and we gon' fight, Nija.

She climbed over the console and started the car. "I need my purse out of my car, my license is in there," she said wiping her face. Opening the driver's door of her ride, I leaned inside and retrieved her purse. "Is he dead?" she asked when I placed the purse on the seat.

"That's not important. Back straight out and drive off. Don't look back and text me when you get to my crib. Pop the trunk for me though,"

Snatching a blanket out the trunk, I closed it and tapped the top of the car twice for her to go. When Nija drove away, I went to work getting the mystery nigga out the middle of the parking lot. Using the blanket to roll him in, I picked his scrawny ass up and walked over to the dumpster. Without a struggle, I lifted his body and threw his ass inside while holding on to a corner of the blanket. It was going with me to the barbeque pit, no evidence of my presence would be left there.

I found a garbage bag in the back of Nija's car and stuffed the blanket inside. After closing the door, I kicked something and looked down. It was the stupid muthafucka's piece. I scooped it up and ran around the car, jumping in. Throwing the car in drive, I peeled out of the preserve without looking back.

Heading to the expressway, I fished my phone out of my pocket and hit up Ricio. I put the phone on speaker and waited for him to answer. His voicemail came on and I snatched my phone up and ended the call. But I called his ass right back.

"Bro, what's up?" he asked irritably.

"Where fuck you at, nigga?"

"I'm at the bank checking out this safe deposit box. I'm also about to open a joint account for both of us for the money that's already here. In other words, I'm working. What's going on, though?"

"I got a situation that I don't want to talk about over the phone. You need to get to my house asap because shit just got real."

"You got to tell me more than that, brah."

"How long are you going to be at the bank? Nija needs you right now," I responded trying not to go into detail.

"Fuck Nija! She called you about our conversation this morning?"

"I don't even know what you're talking about, Ricio. What I'm referring to has nothing to do with a conversation. I had to take out the trash because somebody was following her."

Ricio was quiet for a minute then I heard a door close. "What the fuck you mean somebody was following her? Where is she?"

His attitude toward Nija changed the minute he heard what I said. My brother was far from slow, he knew something drastic happened and staying mad at her was a thing of the past. I'll bet money he was on his way to my house.

"I will tell you more when I get to my house. Nija should be texting me any moment letting me know she made it there."

"Why the fuck is she alone, brah?"

"Nigga I had to clean up! Just get to my shit and stop asking so many questions. I'll fill you in when you get there!"

"I'm on my way. Let me wrap this shit up for another day," he said disconnecting the call.

As soon as I sat the phone on my thigh, Nija texted telling me she was at my crib. I merged onto the expressway and headed to my home. Floyd was closer to laying on his back for eternity with the bullshit he'd concocted.

I pulled up about fifteen minutes later. Stepping out of Nija's car, the door swung open and she ran down the stairs throwing her arms around my neck. I hugged her and she was shaking like she was seizing.

"Calm down, Nija. You're safe now. Come on so you can sit down," I said leading her up the stairs.

"Why was he following me? I'm not beefing with no damn body!" she cried as she entered the living room. "I didn't even know his deranged ass!"

"He said Floyd sent him. Apparently, his brother was killed when Ricio's family chased down the cars at the cemetery. They used you as a way to get at Ricio. I'm glad you were quick to call me. It could've been a different outcome if you hadn't.

He was going to kill you, Nija. Somebody told them where you lived and worked. Tell me what happened at your job today. Maybe it will give insight on some things."

"I was having a good day until lunch. Barbeque is what I wanted and I walked to the restaurant down the street. For some reason I thought I heard someone following me as I walked down the street," she said pausing. "As a matter of fact, he was the guy that talked to me inside the restaurant! He could've killed me then, bro!" she screamed with tears streaming down her face.

"What else happened?"

"When I got back to work, one of my coworkers told me my sister was waiting for me in my office. Nihiyah was sitting behind my desk and we got into a heated argument because I wouldn't give her money. Last week, Kimmie informed me that Nihiyah was on drugs and she was pissed because I refused to give her my hard earned money to put up her nose."

The wheels started turning in my head. The dude said a crack-head gave them the information and I knew damn well Nija's sister didn't put her in harm's way for a hit. Sister or no sister, drugs trumped anything for an addict, even family.

"Nija, do you think your sister set you up?" I asked straight up.

"To be honest, Nihiyah is not the same person I grew up with. To hear you say someone told those men where I worked, I don't fuck with too many females. Nihiyah already had me wondering about her but I didn't want to believe my thoughts. I know this may get my sister killed, but I won't hold on to the information any longer.

Remember when Ricio's truck got shot up?" I shook my head yes and my ears perked up. "I was on the phone with her that day while we were getting food. She asked for money that day too and asked my whereabouts. Thinking nothing of it, I told her. Then minutes later Ricio's dodging bullets and bodying niggas in broad daylight.

There's one more thing I need to tell you. Promise me that nothing will happen to Nihiyah until I talk to my mother," Nija pleaded.

"I can't promise you that, I'm sorry. Your sister wanted to play Russian Roulette with her life, she gotta watch the ball roll. There are no second chances because of her relationship status with you. What else is there to tell, Nija. I have no sympathy for your bum ass sister."

"Nihiyah is fucking with Shake. I found out at the same time I learned she was on drugs."

"She ain't fucking with that nigga right now. He's in the hospital fighting for his life and he won't ever walk out. Nihiyah is delivering information directly to Floyd. Which in turn means, he is the one feeding her dope as compensation."

"Everything you said is making more sense as I keep thinking about it. Nihyah hates Ricio with a passion and it's been showing in the past week or so. She says he put his hands on her or something but I never found out the whole story. All I know is she saw him with some bitch and he put hands on her."

"Nah, it's more than that because Ricio ain't gon' put his hands on a female without probable cause. Nihiyah told half of the fuckin' story," I said taking up for my brother.

"Who the fuck did I hit?" Ricio asked coming into the room.

"Nihiyah," Nija spoke up. "She said you hit her when she saw you with one of your hoes."

"I didn't hit that bitch! I choked the fuck out of her and pushed her on her ass though. Big difference. She's lucky I didn't knock her out the way she was punching me in the back of my head. How the hell did y'all get on that subject anyway?" Ricio asked sitting down looking at Nija.

Sis turned away from him so the tension between the two was thick as fuck. I wasn't concerned about their lover's quarrel and I wasn't questioning neither one about it. All I wanted to do was get to the root of the problem we had at the moment.

"Like I was telling you on the phone, a nigga followed Nija from her job. She called me and I had her to lead him to the forest preserve on 147th and killed his ass after getting some information from him. I found out after talking to Nija, her sister is the person that fed them information on how to find her. The dude was the brother to one of the niggas that died by the hands of Alejandro. Nihiyah is a crackhead and she was fucking with Shake and Floyd in some type of way. She almost had her sister killed and I believe she's the reason Nija is suspended from work." I said explaining the issue in very little detail but with key points.

"I never took your sister as being a mole. Did you ever tell her ass where I laid my head?" Ricio asked Nija.

"No, why would I do something like that? My mama doesn't even know where you live! I was followed to be killed and all you're worried about is your place of residence, pitiful muthafucka," she said standing up with her purse in hand. "Rodrigo, I'm going home. I'll call you when I get there."

"Those niggas know where you live, Nija! It's not safe there for you anymore!" I leaped up blocking her path.

"How thee fuck they know that shit?" Ricio asked.

"Nihiyah!" both me and Nija yelled.

"Ni, your sister just got herself into something that she won't be able to get out of. You ain't going back to that house. You will be staying with me until this is all over."

"The hell I will! I wouldn't stay with you if it was the last place on earth. We are over, Ricio. I will stay with Kimmie, thanks anyway," she said trying to step past me.

"You don't have a choice. Sit down, Ni."

"Muthafuckas are trying to kill me because of all this shit that's going on. I can't go back to work because my fucked up sister wanted to come to my job and start shit. I'm over all of this, Ricio. I'm going to Kimmie's and that's final. Fix this shit so I can get back to living my damn life! Y'all figure this shit out because I'm out."

"Nija—"

"Let her go, bro. Nija call me when you get to Kimmie's and be careful. Everything will be alright, I promise. Stay away from your sister because she's against you. Holla at moms too because she will definitely have to bury her daughter," I said giving her a hug.

"As much as I love my sister, she brought this on herself. There's nothing I can do about it. I just want to give my mom a heads up about her daughter first. I love you, bro and thanks for being there for me today," she said before leaving.

Ricio stood at the window watching Nija get into her car. I ran to the door and down the stairs. "Nija!" I yelled before she could back out of the driveway. I went to the back seat and grabbed the garbage bag. "Drive safely and watch yourself out here," I said closing the door. Ricio was waiting for me in the doorway as I climbed the stairs.

"What's in the bag, bro?"

"The blanket I used to wrap that nigga in to get his ass inside the dumpster. I'm about to burn this muthafucka in the barbeque pit." I said. We may as well sit, smoke, and figure out what we're about to do," I said walking toward the patio door with Ricio behind me.

Meesha

Chapter 8
Beast

The things that's been going on in the past couple weeks were hitting everybody hard. Floyd sent them niggas to get at us at our most vulnerable time. It was a blessing that no one was seriously hurt. Sin getting hit made my heart stop instantly. But I've been going through hell with her because I won't let her roam the streets to look for the muthafuckas.

I was sitting in my La-Z-Boy recliner watching Richard Pryor's documentary on *Netflix* while Sin was in the laundry room putting in a load of clothes. She had hardly said three words to me since last week but she'd be alright. As long as there was food on the table and she was alive and well, she didn't have to say shit to me ever again.

"Beast! Sin!" Madysen screamed from the guest bedroom.

Jumping up, I raced down the hall and Sin was right behind me. When I went into the room, Madysen was nowhere to be found. Sin ran to the other side of the bed and she wasn't there either.

"Help me!" Madysen screamed out.

I raced out of the room and ran to the bathroom. Pushing the door open, Madysen was lying on her side in a fetal position holding her stomach. Tears were rolling down her face and a huge puddle of water was under her body.

"What's going on, Mads?"

"My water broke! It hurts so bad!" she cried.

Sin walked to the door with a confused look on her face. "It's too early for you to have contractions, Madysen. Get up so we can go to the hospital."

"I don't think I can walk. It hurts too much."

"Beast pick her up and take her to the car. I'll call Dr. Langstein and tell her what's going on."

Doing as Sin asked, I bent down and scooped Madysen into my arms and grabbed a couple towels before leaving the bathroom. When we got inside the garage, I stood her on her feet while I placed the towels on the backseat. She wasn't getting all that baby residue on my fucking seats.

"Come on, Madysen sit on the towels. We'll be at the hospital in no time. When was your last contraction?"

"I don't know!" she screamed.

"Okay let me know when another one comes so I can start timing them," I said going to the driver's side of the car.

Starting the car, I kept looking in the rearview mirror as I waited on Sin to come out of the house. I honked the horn a few times to let her know she needed to come the fuck on. Sin emerged from the house and snatched the door open with aggression. She was about to start bitching about something.

"Madysen, what the fuck is this?" She asked holding out a bottle of castor oil as she sat in the passenger seat of the car.

"I couldn't poop and I took a couple tablespoons last night and more this morning," Madysen said.

"Are you serious? You forced yourself to go into labor, Madysen!"

"Madysen, you should've said something to one of us. That could be dangerous for the baby and you for that matter," I said backing out of the garage.

"I'm tired of being pregnant! I'm not going to lie to y'all I looked up how to go into labor on the internet and came across Castor oil. I said I didn't want this baby and I was forced to carry it! Blame yourselves for forcing me to do something I didn't want to do! I don't care!" she exclaimed.

"Bitch! I'll beat yo' muthafuckin' ass in this car!" Sin yelled jumping up in the seat turning around to look Madysen in the eyes. "You have been one selfish muthafucka since the day you found out about that baby! For you to claim to love my nephew so much, you sure are adamant about getting rid of this baby! Is it his? Tell me now because if it's not, I'm fuckin' you up!"

"Sit the fuck down, Sincere! Yo' ass always jumping to conclusions and I'm tired of it! The girl has been through a lot in the past couple weeks. She watched the father of her baby, your nephew, get murdered in front of her. You are the one that's being insensitive about *her* feelings. Enough is enough, dammit!"

"Erique—"

"Shut the fuck up! I don't want to hear shit else out of you, Sin! Yes, she was wrong for drinking that shit. What's done is done and there's nothing we can do about it. The baby is coming regardless."

All the bickering back and forth between them was tearing me and Sin apart. Something had to change because I wasn't about to live my life being the referee of their fight matches. Sin was going to have to calm the fuck down because she was being too tough on the damn girl. My phone started buzzing, I picked it up and answered it.

"Yeah."

"Aye, Beast, some shit went down today that I want to run by you," Ricio said in my ear.

"I'm on my way to Northwestern Memorial because Madysen is in labor. I'll hit you when I get there, I have to concentrate on the road."

"It's too early though," he said.

"I know. I'll explain shit when I call you back."

"Nah, me and Rodrigo are on our way. See you in a minute."

"Who was that?" Sin asked

"Ricio. Him and Rodrigo is on their way to the hospital. Call Nija and tell her what's going on," I said without looking at her.

Madysen was moaning and groaning fifteen minutes into the drive to the hospital. I was praying she wasn't in active labor in my shit. That was going to be a heavy-duty detail for my ride. We still had about another ten minutes before we made it to the hospital. Traffic was flowing and I was speeding.

"Beast, it feels like this baby is coming out!" Madysen screamed from the backseat.

"Not in this muthafucka, it won't! Sin see what the fuck is going on back there."

Sin climbed to the back to check on Madysen and she wasn't saying shit at first. I was nervous because her water had already broken back at the house.

"She's crowning, Beast. This baby is about to come whether you want it to or not," Sin said in a shaky voice. "I've never delivered a baby but I will if I have to."

"We are almost at the hospital. Don't push that baby out, Madysen!" I said pushing on the gas. I didn't give a fuck about the police, that baby was not coming in my car.

"I gotta push! It feels like I have to shit!" Madysen screamed. "Oh my God, I gotta push!"

"Wait Madysen, don't push. I see the head a little bit but every time you scream it goes back up. Calm down and push long and hard without screaming," Sin coached.

"Sin I just said she ain't having that baby in my ride, man!" I screamed not taking my eyes off the road. "The hospital is two exits away."

"And this baby will be here before you get there. Push Madysen," I heard Sin say. "One, two, three, four—"

"Aaaaaaarrrrghhhhh!" Madysen screamed after pushing for four seconds.

"Come on Madysen, stop screaming and just push. The head is out. On the count of three push again and don't stop until I get to ten. One, two, three, push!" Every time Sin said push, I cringed. "Oh my God, stop pushing Madysen, the cord is around the neck."

The car was so quiet I stopped breathing while I waited to learn what happened. It seemed like forever before I heard Sin's voice again. The sign for the hospital was in front of me and I rushed to get to the building.

"Okay, I got it, push one more time and your baby will be here, Madysen." Sin cried out.

When I pulled in front of the emergency room, the sound of a baby crying filled the car and I let out the breath I was holding. I jumped out of the car and went inside to get help.

"Help me, my niece just delivered a baby in the car!" I screamed running back out the door. Opening the back door, Madysen had the baby wrapped in one of the towels I had place under her.

"It's a boy and there's no denying who his father is," Madysen said smiling as she moved the towel down for me to see.

The lil nigga looked just like Max's ass. I was too gangsta to cry in public so I held that shit back and pumped my fist as I pointed toward the sky. Max planted his seed and left his legacy here for us to enjoy.

"Excuse me sir, I need to get to the mother and child, please," a nurse said from behind me with a wheelchair.

Stepping aside I let them do their job as they got Madysen and the baby out of the car. Sin got out behind her and I leaned in to see how much damage was done to my shit. Seeing the blood on the towel I almost threw the fuck up and backed out.

"Sin, get this towel out of my car."

"Go park the car and get back here," she said rushing inside the hospital behind the wheelchair that held Madysen.

***

"What up, Beast," Ricio called out as I was getting out of the car. "Did she have the baby yet?"

"Hell yeah, she had that lil muthafucka, right in the backseat of my car!" I said when he got closer.

"Damn Unc, you sound mad," Rodrigo laughed.

"I've got blood all over my damn seat. Even though it's leather, I still know its blood back there. Look at that muthafuckin' towel, man. I'm not touching that shit."

"What did she have?" Ricio asked.

Tears sprang to my eyes because I was there when Max was born and when I saw Madysen's son, it took me back to that day. Knowing I will never see him again hurt my heart. I hadn't cried one time since Max died, but I finally did on the day his son was born.

"She had a boy and he look just like his daddy, man. Shit is fucked up because he should be here to celebrate this day with us. I swear, them niggas gon' pay for taking him from us," I sobbed.

Both Ricio and Rodrigo hugged me because they knew I had been holding back my feelings. Taking my moment to cry, I sucked that shit up and wiped my face. Staring up at the sky, I smiled. I knew my niggas Reese and Max was smiling down right along with me.

"Aight, what y'all got for me?" I asked cleaning my face. I wasn't about all that crying shit plus they had news for me.

"Them niggas went after Nija today. If it wasn't for her quick thinking, she might not be here. I had to set a trap and I murdered that muthafucka. Left his ass stankin' in the dumpster of a forest preserve," Rodrigo said.

"Who was it?"

"I don't know who the nigga was. He said his brother was one of the niggas that Alejandro hit after the burial. He told us how he knew where Nija would be and I shot his ass up."

So, who's feeding these muthafuckas information? Don't tell me we got a mole in the crew," I said folding my arms over my chest.

"Nah, it's Nija's sister who told Floyd that shit. Her stupid ass didn't know shit else so she had them to go after Nija to get to Ricio. Her ass just signed her own death certificate though. I don't give a fuck who she is," Rodrigo said.

"She should've done research on the street code, that's on her. What is Nija's thoughts on what her sister did?" I asked.

"Nija is pissed because she could've died today. Then to make matters worse, Nihiyah was the one that set up the drive by I was involved in a couple weeks ago. Her ass has to go before somebody dies because of her reckless ass." Ricio said.

"I agree but we have to scope these niggas out and see how they're moving. Rodrigo, you put us in a position where we can't move around like we want to because of your little five minutes of fame on live tv. If we start killing muthafuckas left and right, that will bring a lot of heat our way. I think we should get the product out in these streets.

All of Reese's traps are still in tip top shape. I have been getting them ready for operation and in a week or so, things should be set. We will talk about it more once we set up a meeting."

"I went to the bank to check out the safe deposit box. Reese left his boys good. I don't think we need to use the traps because I'm not trying to be a trap boy. We gon' put bricks on the street. I'll take over by providing the product to these niggas for less than what they are already paying. Not to mention, the product is better too."

"We will discuss this in the meeting. I'll set it up and get in touch with y'all. I want to go up and check on Madysen and the baby," I said walking toward the hospital.

"The city of Chicago is about to be bloody as fuck. Don't take too long because you know how I get when I need to kill," Rodrigo said walking ahead of me.

Meesha

Chapter 9
Latorra

What I experienced at the prison with James Carter, really messed up my psyche. Hearing him talk about knowing my mom and grandma had my heart fluttering. I've wished for the longest time to find someone who knew about my family. Being alone without anyone has been a real struggle for me. He put so much on my mind, I didn't know what to do with it.

I called off work because I couldn't face him again at that point. All the shit I'd been through early on in my life and I had a father that I didn't know anything about. One that was locked up in the very prison where I worked. At the same time, he may not be my dad, but he wanted a DNA test to prove it.

Holding the piece of paper that James gave me in my hand for the hundredth time since Wednesday, I looked at it contemplating if I should make the call. His sister, Lynetta, didn't know me from a can of paint but he wanted me to call her. I stood up from the bed and went into the bathroom to relieve my bladder. My phone started ringing from the bedroom, whoever it was would have to wait.

As I washed my hands, my phone rang again. I raced back to my room and snatched it up. "Hello."

"What's up Miss Smith? How's things going with you?" Mauricio said in his deep baritone.

"Everything is everything. Sorry I didn't make it to your brother's service, I had to work. How are you?" I asked with a smile on my face.

"It's all good, ma. I made it through just fine, don't beat yourself up about that. As for me, I'm living day by day and I'm a proud uncle as of yesterday."

"Congratulations! They say when one life is taken another is born. I'm happy for your family," I said happily.

"I wanna see you, Miss Smith. Where you at?" he asked.

"I'm at home."

"Can a nigga come see you or nah?" he laughed.

"Yeah, I'm up for company. I'll text the address when we get off the phone."

"I'm driving now, send that and I'll see you shortly, ma," he said hanging up.

I hurriedly sent him my address and ran to the bathroom to freshen up. Ricio coming to my house meant I was about to get the dick I've been craving. Just what the doctor ordered to get my mind off the bullshit that's been going on in my life. I would make my decision about the phone call later.

Slipping on a pair of booty shorts and a tank, I laid back on my bed thinking about how his hands would feel on my body. The thought of sexing him was always on my mind and I was ready to put it in motion. I hadn't seen him in a while and I looked forward to him coming over. We may not become an item, but that didn't mean we couldn't have fun and enjoy one another.

The doorbell rang and I damn near broke my neck getting to the pad on the wall. I tripped over the end table stubbing my toe. The pain was running up my leg but I wasn't about to let that stop nothing. "Who is it?" I asked pushing the talk button on the intercom. I quickly pushed the listen button to hear the response of whomever was downstairs.

"It's me, Miss Smith," Ricio replied.

"Come to the second floor," I said buzzing him in. His footsteps made the wood creak with every step he took. Ricio appeared on the other side of the door looking good as hell. He licked his lips and my pussy drooled.

"Open the door, Smith. I see your eye covering the damn peephole. Stop admiring a nigga from afar and let me in," he laughed.

"Damn, he caught my ass," I said to myself as I unlocked the door. I stepped aside letting him in, he looked me over and wrapped his arms around my waist.

"How you doing, ma?" He asked letting me go. "You looking mighty scrumptious in those shorts. You didn't have to work today?" he asked looking down at me.

"I did but I called off," I said limping to toward the couch.

"What's wrong with your leg?" he asked as he sat down.

"The damn table stuck it's leg out and I hit my toe."

"Yo' ass was rushing to get to a nigga, huh?"

"Whatever, that shit hurt. I think I broke it," I said looking down at my foot.

"Put it up here so I can take a look at it." he said patting his thigh.

As he examined my toe like he was an orthopedic doctor, I gazed at the side of his face wondering what the hairs on his face would look like with my juices coating them. His plump lips wrapped around my clit with my legs spread wide, was the image I saw before me. My pussy thumped with every beat of my heart.

"Ouch, fool, that shit hurts!" I screamed as he wiggled my toe back and forth.

"Shut yo' cry baby ass up. I was trying to make sure you didn't break that ugly muthafucka. You didn't answer my question, how you doing?" he asked massaging my foot.

"I'm okay, can't complain. How are you holding up?"

"Shit is hard and I miss the hell out of my brother, but I couldn't cry over it too long. There's so much I have to get in motion and I need a leveled head to get it done."

"Please don't go out seeking revenge, it's not worth it, Ricio."

"My brother will get justice and I'm not talking about from the law. I'm not trying to hear none of that shit, all them niggas going down. If it takes the rest of my life, he will get justice. He didn't get the opportunity to live because of them niggas! Look, I didn't come over here to talk about me. I haven't seen you since the last time we went out and I wanted to make sure you were good."

"I'm alright. I just needed a break from that prison. It's depressing watching strong black men getting broken down by the system. The things that goes on in there shouldn't be happening but I go in, do my job and go home. It's a job and that's all that matters to me," I said holding my head down. 'Call my sister, Yvette' echoed through my mind.

"What's wrong, Smith?"

"Ricio call me Latorra. Using my last name takes me back to my job and I'm trying to be far away from there this weekend.

Nothing is wrong, but everything isn't alright either. I don't want to talk about it," I said removing my foot from his lap leaning in to kiss his lips.

I felt the hesitation in his movement as I parted his lips with my tongue. He finally opened up and kissed me back. His hand moved to my ass when I deepened the kiss. Closing my eyes, I sucked on his bottom lip and a groan escaped his throat. He pulled back and looked into my eyes.

"Don't start something you don't plan on finishing, nah," he smirked.

"The only way we won't finish is if you back out. I've been thinking about this dick since you called. I want it," I said running my hand along the front of his pants.

When I felt his hand move from my ass to between my legs, I knew things were about to get steamy. His fingers strummed my clit through my shorts and my head instantly dropped to his chest. My breathing became heavy and my eyes rolled to the top of my head. The moisture that flowed from my kitty slid down the crack of my ass making me change the position I was in.

Ricio gently pushed me back onto the couch with his free hand without removing his fingers from my pearl. Easing my shorts down over my hips, I knew he was about to feast on my goodies. Tossing my shorts behind his back, Ricio stood tall and pulled a gold wrapper from his pocket and unbuckled his pants. When he pulled his boxers down my eyes lit up at the sight of his dick. That piece of work hung mid thigh and it was beautiful.

He tore the condom open with his teeth and slid it on slowly. Never taking his eyes off me. Ricio eased onto the couch and pried my legs open with his knees. My excitement went down a notch because there wasn't any oral foreplay as I expected. Nudging my legs wider, he leaned down and kissed me.

His tip penetrated my opening and I gasped. Ricio was working with a monster and his girth was nothing to play with. Stroking long and slow before he raised my legs to my ears and moved in and out of me faster.

"Shit! Sssssssss," I hissed as he massaged my honey dew walls.

"This what you've been waiting for, huh?" he asked thrusting harder into my kitty. "I've been thinking about this gushy since the first time I laid eyes on you. I knew your shit was gon' be good and I was right, with your sexy ass."

Ricio wasn't fucking me, he was making love to the pussy. I was clawing at his back and couldn't find my voice to respond. The only thing I could do was moan and pop my kitty against him.

"I'm cummin', shit!"

"Me too, ma. Let that shit go, Fuck!" he growled as his pipe became harder and his back stiffened as he pressed forward one last time. His back was rigid and he was stuck for a few seconds before he fell forward without applying all of his weight on my small frame. "Where's your bathroom?" he asked as he planted one foot on the floor and stood.

Rolling my eyes, I got up behind him and pointed down the hall. "First door on the left." I didn't wait to see if he found it or not. I was low-key pissed because what I thought was a special moment, turned out to be me getting fucked and left with a wet ass.

I cursed myself all the way to my bedroom for initiating that shit. Now, he was going to start treating me like one of his hoes. I didn't want to be part of that category but I'd placed myself right in the midst of the list.

"Aye Smith—I mean Latorra! Where you at, ma?" Ricio called out.

"I'm right here," I said walking into the hall.

"Thanks for letting a nigga slide through. I gotta head out, I'll call you later. I have some business to attend to, it was good seeing you." I stared at him with my forehead scrunched up and a mug on my face. "What's wrong?" he asked.

I checked myself quickly because I wasn't about to let him know how I was affected by his actions. "Nothing, everything's cool. I'll talk to you later," I said walking to the door and opened it.

"Damn, I don't get a hug or shit, huh?"

"My bad, I'm tired and want to take a shower and lay down for a minute," I lied as I opened my arms for him to get his hug.

"Aight, I'll holla at you. Keep it tight for me," he said running his hand along my slit. "Stop looking sad too, I'll be back," he kissed me on the cheek, leaving me standing there.

After locking up behind Ricio, I showered and took a nap as planned. I slept for about three hours waking up wondering if I should make the call to James' sister or not. Did I want to know if this man was my father? I asked myself. It really didn't matter because I was grown and the rough part of my life was behind me. The thought of having living relatives was better than being in this fucked up world alone.

I got out of bed and walked over to the dresser and picked up my phone and the piece of paper with Lynette's number on it. Sitting in the chair that was in front of my bedroom window, I glanced out and the sky was dreary just like my mood. At that moment the urge to throw the number away was strong. Instead, I looked at the phone and dialed the number placing it on speaker as I waited for someone to answer.

"Hello."

"Hi, may I speak with Lynette, please?" I asked nervously.

"This is she, who's calling?"

"My name is Latorra. Your brother James Carter gave me your number—"

"I've been waiting days for you to call me. So, you're Rosalind's daughter, huh? Do you know how long we've been looking for y'all?"

"No, I don't. James said he's been looking for my mother but what I don't understand is how y'all didn't know she was dead. Her death was all over the news and in the papers, everybody knew about it, except y'all. That's where the confusion comes in with me."

"I remember the story but I didn't put two and two together because a picture was never displayed when it was mentioned. The segments only mentioned it briefly. I understand why you would have doubts and I don't know what type of life you lived after the ordeal. My brother really wants to know if you are his daughter and so do I. He loved Roz with all his heart and was never the same when her mother moved her away from him."

I listened to what Lynette said but in the back of my mind, I felt there was more to why James wanted to find out if he was my daddy. "I doubt if I'm his daughter. My mother never mentioned your brother and I'd never heard of him until the day he stepped to me at the prison. I will take the test just to prove him wrong, but I don't know where things will go afterward.

I've been on my own too long so, happiness is something I'm not feeling at the moment. I basically want to get this over and done with. No disrespect to you or him, but I don't know y'all. I don't trust nobody in this fucked up world we live in. Excuse my French."

"We can let things play out as they may when the time comes. For now, we will concentrate on getting the test done and wait on the results. You haven't quit your job over this have you?" she asked.

"No, why would you ask that?"

"Well Jim has been looking for you at the prison. He mentioned that he hasn't seen you in the past couple days and he was afraid you'd quit."

"I took a couple days off to process the news he sprang on me. I don't work on weekends so I won't be back to work until next week."

"I've scheduled an appointment for Monday to get the test done. Will that be good for you?"

"Actually no, I have to work Monday morning. How will James get out to take the test?" I asked confused."

"I actually paid the fee for the Diagnostic physician to go get a sample from him at the prison. They are waiting for you to go down and give your sample so they can run the test. It will take probably thirty minutes to an hour and you'll be done. Then after that, we wait."

"Send the address to me and I'll be there Monday," I said ready to get off the phone.

"Okay, I can do that. Save my number in your phone because I would love to keep in contact with you. There's no doubt in my mind that you are the baby Rosalind was carrying from my brother. Time will tell, I'll talk to you later, Latorra."

"Yeah, time will tell," I said ending the call.

Chapter 10
Floyd

Searching high and low for this crackhead bitch on the Westside, I was fuming. Money hadn't been heard from since I sent him to Ricio's bitch's job. The last I heard from him was when he called saying he was tailing her ass. I ain't heard shit since and the bitch can't be dead because the news hadn't reported any homicides involving females.

Driving down Madison I saw Nihiyah standing in front of White Castle. Whipping my shit damn near on the curb, I threw my car in park. She looked up and took off running. Throwing the car in drive I cut into the alley that I saw her enter and pushed the petal all the way to the floor board. I caught up with her in no time and clipped her with the side of the bumper. Just enough to make her lose her balance.

I jumped out of my car and ran around the vehicle, collaring her ass by her shirt. "What the fuck happened the other day, bitch?" I growled in her face. "Where the fuck is Money?"

"I don't know what happened, I swear. Money was still outside in his car when I left my sister's job. He gave me some money and a pack and told me to catch the bus where I wanted to go. His exact words to me were, 'I got it from here, you did good,' and I left. Why the fuck you coming at me like I did something wrong? The only thing I've done was get you closer to your target."

"I haven't heard from Money! You better hope he is good or yo' ass going down for whatever happened to him. Where the fuck is yo' sister? Have you seen her?"

"Nope. I've tried to avoid her because I think she may be fired after the bullshit I pulled at her job. Floyd, you didn't say nothing about hurting my sister. I told you she was the way to get to Ricio, that's all."

"Bitch, you don't run what the fuck I do! I do whatever it takes with the information that's given to me. I'm not responsible for the shit that happens to a muthafucka, they should pick the people they fuck with carefully. Your sister is on my radar because she was the last bitch in my nigga presence and he's nowhere to be found.

I don't give a fuck what you gotta do, find her ass and find out where the fuck she at and report back to me! Is that understood? If I don't hear back from yo' hype ass, I'm killing you on sight. Don't fuck with me Nihiyah! For the record, there's no backing out, you in this shit to the end. Keep ya mouth closed unless you're talking to me," I growled as I shoved her into a pile of garbage and jumped in my whip, peeling off.

Shit had been falling apart and I didn't know where to start to fix it. Half of our Westside crew was gone. Ricio and his mutha-fuckin' crew was killing any and everybody associated with me and Big Jim. I was out here trying to survive without Shake, he was fighting a battle that was between him and God at that point.

Rod was missing in action and wasn't answering his phone. I needed him to get on the case and get the big homie Big Jim out of that muthafuckin' prison. He needed to help regulate the shit that was going on. All the weight was being put on my shoulders and it was weighing me down heavily.

The truth coming out about Reese's death fucked the operation up badly. I knew shit would come out eventually but I wasn't expecting anything of this caliber. Both Big Jim and myself underestimated Reese's sons and they were coming for us hard.

Jumping on the expressway, I kept checking my surroundings because Sosa's ass could be anywhere. That nigga wasn't as vicious when he ran in the streets alongside us. He put in work but it was nothing compared to what he had been doing lately.

Traffic was moving but not fast enough. I had to get to the crib so I could get the monkey off my back to ease my mind. The hospital was where I needed to be but I was going to take a nap beforehand so I could be alert. The last time I was there, Shake was on a ventilator and couldn't breathe on his own. His doctor told me about all of his wounds and my nigga was fucked up.

A bullet had penetrated his large intestines and lodged in his lung. They were able to remove it but he would have to wear a shit bag for the rest of his life. His left leg was shattered and they had to use screws, plates, and metal rods to hold his bones in place.

Shake was lucky as hell that the shot to his head only grazed him and took off the tip of his ear. Somebody upstairs in heaven was looking out for his ass because had it connected, he wouldn't even be laid up in a hospital bed. His ass would've gone straight to the morgue with a fitted toe tag.

As I turned onto my street, I noticed a detective's car parked a few feet from my house. Pulling into the driveway, I cut the engine, got out and went straight to the mailbox. Stalling to see what they were on, I started looking through the junk mail as I slowly made my way up the walkway. Hearing the sound of car doors closing simultaneously, I turned around and waited for them to get closer to me.

"Floyd Douglas?" one of the detectives asked taking his sunglasses off.

"Yeah, I'm him. What brings you to my house?"

"I'm Detective Bradley and this is my partner Detective Cooper. We need to talk to you about Attorney Rodney Banks."

"What about him?" I asked in confusion. Rod had been unreachable for days and now these muthafuckas were at my doorstep wanting to talk about his ass.

"Records indicates Mr. Banks was the attorney representing your homie James Carter in his murder case. Your name came up as the person that conducted business on Mr. Carter's behalf. When was the last time you talked to Mr. Banks?"

I didn't know where he was going with his line of questioning and using Rod's name in a past tense didn't sit well with me. I knew damn well nothing happened because I hadn't heard shit. Glancing between both men without saying anything, I tried to come up with my own interpretation of what was going on.

"Did you hear what he asked you, boy?" Detective Cooper asked rudely.

"First of all, you know my name, nigga. I ain't been nobody's boy in a long ass time, I'm a grown man! Secondly, I don't appreciate you sayin' that shit when you address me because in my eyes, that's a racial slur coming from a white muthafucka!"

"I didn't ask you shit about any of that, answer the fucking question, motherfucker!" Cooper yelled with his hand on his gun.

"You come to my house and got the nerve to think ya'll gon' talk to me any kind of way! Slavery been dead and I don't give a fuck who you are. In order to get respect, you got to give it. If you not here to arrest my black ass, get the fuck off my property," I said walking toward my house.

"Mr. Douglas, I apologize on my partner's behalf, would you please give me a few minutes of your time?" Detective Bradley asked nicely.

Stepping on the bottom step I paused. I took a deep breath before I turned around glaring at the bitch ass Detective named Cooper. "If whatever you came to discuss is going to be turned around and pinned on me, I'm not saying shit!"

"Nothing will go against you, Floyd. I'm only trying to find out what happened to Mr. Banks. With you being associated with him, I figured you could give me a timeline on his last known whereabouts," Detective Bradley tried to reassure me.

"I've been trying to contact him to talk about Mr. Carter's case since last week but he hasn't been answering his phone. We have an appointment for Tuesday so I figured I'd wait until then to talk about the things I have questions about. I've told you all I know. So, can you tell me what's really going on, Detective Bradley?"

"Well last week Friday there was a call about a house fire in Englewood. Attorney Banks was found in the rubble and had to be identified through dental records. Is it a coincidence that Mr. Banks was burned in his home the same day his son was shot?"

"His son?" I asked puzzled.

"Yeah, Rodney Banks Jr. known on the street as Shake," Cooper said walking up behind Bradley. "Don't say you don't know him because you have been to the hospital on more than one occasion. You're the one that told the doctors to use an alias in case the people that shot him tried looking for him."

"I used that story because all I knew him as was Shake! I didn't know his real fuckin' name and I damn sure didn't know he was Rodney's son! Get the fuck outta here with that bullshit," I said waving my hand at his goofy ass. "As a matter fact, don't say shit else to me. Rodney's death don't have nothing to do with what happened to Shake!"

"The hospital now has his real name on file. We went to check on him, your buddy is not doing too good, Mr. Douglas. What exactly happened to the young Mr. Banks?" Bradley asked calmly.

"I don't know," I lied.

"Oh, you know!" Cooper shouted. "You niggers are tearing up the city with all of your gunfire and want to use the code of silence to deal with the shit yourselves! How many more people have to die before you idiots let us do our jobs?"

"Bitch, you used that word too loosely, take that gun and badge off and we can handle this shit accordingly! You cracker ass muthafuckas don't realize we ain't our ancestors, you will get fucked up!" I said angrily walking toward him.

Cooper instantly snatched his gun from his holster and aimed it at me. "Don't take another step, boy! I'll blow your fuckin' head off!"

"That's all they teach y'all at the academy I see. To pull ya muthafuckin' weapon first, huh? If I was white, you wouldn't be threatened by me, but since my skin is dark, I get treated like a fuckin' animal. You the one that became aggressive towards me but here I am with a fuckin' gun pointed in my face. The America fuckin' way nowadays," I said shaking my head.

"I don't know shit about what happened to Rodney, this is the first I've heard about it," I said to Bradley. "There was no news coverage about the shit. But if he was a white attorney, the shit would've been plastered on every muthafuckin' news station and on the front page of every newspaper.

Y'all pick and choose what to report but want to come to the hood to piece shit together. Fuck y'all! If I'm not being arrested, I'm done talking. Tell ya *boy* to lower his weapon because without it he ain't shit. I'm going into my house now, get the fuck off my property," I said waiting for them to leave.

Bradley reached in his inside pocket and produced a card and held it out to me. "If you hear anything give me a call. I'll be in touch so don't try to leave town anytime soon."

Snatching the card, I looked over at Cooper and smirked. "Get the fuck away from my shit," I said backing up. "Like I said before, I don't know shit."

"Let's get out of here Coop. Floyd, we got our eye on you," Bradley said walking off.

Cooper lowered his gun and walked backwards until he got to the sidewalk, then he turned and followed Bradley to the car. I couldn't believe Rodney was dead. There was no way Big Jim was going to get out now. We had to get another attorney to go over his whole case and he wasn't going to like this shit one bit. I walked up the steps looking over my shoulder before I went in to get high as hell.

Chapter 11
Ricio

Staring at little Max was déjà vu. He looked just like my brother when he was a baby and it was a hard pill to swallow knowing I would never see him again in the flesh. Sin and Beast were gushing over the baby and Rodrigo even softened up for the lil nigga. But Madysen hadn't held him since they made it to the room. Come to think about it, she hasn't said anything to nobody.

"Mads, you good, sis?" I asked. "That was wild that you had that baby in the back of Beast's ride."

"I'm just glad it's over. That shit didn't feel good at all," she said without turning to face me. "I want to get some sleep because my body hurts all over."

"I'm about to dip out to take care of some business but I think Sin and Beast will be here for a minute. Are you going to at least hold him, Madysen?" I asked softly.

"Nah, have them to take him to the nursery when y'all get ready to leave. I don't know how long I'll be sleeping and I don't want him to be awake crying and I don't hear him."

"You need to bond with this baby. Madysen you haven't held him since you got out of the back of the car and that was yesterday. What's the matter with you?" Sin asked.

"Sin, don't start that right now, okay? She is going through a lot right now," Beast said scolding her nicely. "This is not the time."

"She needs to talk about why she took the Castrol oil because I'm not believing the story she told back at the house. She was trying to have this baby before he was ready to come, I'll bet money on it," Sin said cutting her eyes at Madysen.

"I said, this ain't the fuckin' time, Sincere!" Beast barked. "There's a time and place for shit. Listen to me for once and stop trying to be so damn combative. You won't win got dammit!"

That was my cue to leave because I agreed with Beast. Sin was constantly going in on Madysen knowing her mindset. One thing I didn't want was Madysen feeling like we didn't care about her.

Post-partum depression was real and there's been plenty of mother's that took that shit out on the baby.

"Beast I'm about to get out of here. I'll call and check on you later, Madysen. Sin, can I holla at you in the hall?" I asked after hugging Madysen even though she didn't return it. Sin handed the baby to Beast and walked out of the room. "Unc, keep yo' cool, I'm about to talk to her."

"She's going to make me go upside her muthafuckin head," he said in a low growl. "Madysen don't need all the negative tongue lashing from Sin. It's not healthy for her when she's constantly saying she wants to die. The shit is really getting on my nerves," Beast said looking down at the baby.

"This baby is going to need his mother. He will forever have us, but Madysen needs to be a major part of his life as well. We can't force that upon her, she has to be given time to adjust."

"I agree with you on everything you have spoken on. That's the reason I'm going to talk to Sin. I don't want y'all to fall apart because of this. The love that you two have for each other is unbreakable and this won't change that."

I felt like a man older than my years to be talking to someone I've looked up to all my life and speaking to him about handling this shit. Being taught right from wrong, even though I haven't practiced it, I didn't want the two of them bumping heads over the situation that's been placed before us. All three of them had to come to an understanding on how things were going to be from there on out.

"I hear you, Ricio. I don't want nothing to trigger Madysen to do anything stupid to herself or this little boy. I'm trying to keep the peace, that's all. It may seem like I'm taking sides, I'm not. I want what's best for Max's family and to make sure Madysen stays in the right frame of mind to care for him to the best of her ability. With all of us standing behind her, she'll be straight."

"She gon' be good, I'm gon' make sure of it," Rodrigo said before leaving.

"I'll catch you later, Beast," I said looking at the baby once more before I leaned in and kissed him on the forehead. "I love you, nephew. We gotta name you soon, but don't worry we got you."

When I stepped out into the hall, Rodrigo and Sin was already deep in discussion.

"Beast is babying her ass and she's feeding off him saving her. She hasn't even looked at that baby! She drank fucking Castor oil to go in labor, who the fuck does something like that?" Sin fumed.

"I know you are upset but you also have to understand how Madysen is feeling, Sin. She just went through something that was very traumatic. Max basically died in her arms, man," Rodrigo said trying to get Sin to see things his way.

"It was traumatic for everybody, we were all there," she shot back. "We were affected just as much as she was."

"Sin, we were there but we didn't see that shit happen. We were trying to kill them muthafuckas. We witnessed the aftermath of it all, Madysen saw that shit firsthand. To find out you're pregnant after the love of your life is killed breaks the strongest muthafucka," I cut in.

"All she talks about is not wanting to be alive anymore. I'm sick of hearing that shit. Madysen is a mother now. The baby should've given her a different aspect on life. Instead, I feel it made her withdraw even more into herself.

Do you know how many people dream about having kids and here her selfish ass is laying in there contemplating killing herself. I won't allow her to bring no more pain to this family. I swear on everything I love I will beat her ass. If she doesn't want him, I will gladly raise him and she can go about her business."

"Sin, that's not what we want, she has a right to be a part of his life just as much as we do. I really need you to try harder to keep your cool with her," she opened her mouth to make a rebuttal but I held my hand up to stop her from speaking. "Hear me out. You have to spoon feed her until her mind is on the right track. Eat that shit and try harder to get her to feel the love that we're dishing out.

If you don't want to do it for Madysen, do it for baby Max and his daddy. You of all people know how much this means to all of us. I think we've been through enough heartbreak in the last couple of years, especially in the past couple weeks. There's enough bullshit we have to deal with outside of our circle, we don't need chaos within the home front too," I said hopefully putting a little bit on her mind to think about.

"I'll try but I'm not making any promises. I'm still pissed about the shit she did to go into labor. She could've hurt that baby, Ricio."

"But she didn't! He's alright, Sin. Be the bigger person and leave that shit alone for now. Madysen needs you, she needs us more than ever during this time. Stop the pressure and suck it up, okay?" Rodrigo asked holding her hand in his. "I love you but your words have been pretty harsh and it can push her over the edge. If that happens, we, me and you gon' be at odds. I promise you that."

"I'm not worried about that. I said I would try. That's all I can do," she said dropping his hand. "Go take care of your business and I'll see y'all later," she said turning to make her way back to the room.

"Aye, Sin," I called out to her. She turned slightly but never stopped walking. "I love you, auntie. Nothing will ever change that."

"I love you too. Watch yourself out there and be careful."

"This shit gon' get worse before it gets better. I hope Sin don't kill that girl," Rodrigo said leading the way out of the hospital. "Where the fuck we going anyway?"

"I'm about to ride around to look for Slim. There's a reason Reese mentioned him so he knows something about what the fuck is going on. I'm ready to find out too. Oh, before I forget. Monday you have to go to the bank and sign off on the paperwork so you'll have full access to the accounts I set up. We're in this shit together and I don't want you to be in the dark about nothing.

I also found a crib for Angel not too far from you because he's adamant about not going back to the DR. Alejandro fucked up with that nigga but he fits right in with us so he should be cool. Remember that cat Sam that runs shit up north, that nigga hit my line asking if I could hook him up with a connect. That shit was music to my ears. We will be meeting up with him tomorrow along with Angel since he will be rolling with us now."

"Damn nigga, did you have to say all that shit at once? I didn't get a chance to speak on nothing," Rodrigo stated.

"I had to get that shit out while it was fresh on my mind. Speak yo' piece nigga, we about to be rolling for a minute. It's hard as hell to track down a fiend in these streets."

"You got that shit right. But Angel will be alright and I heard all the other things you mentioned. I'm all for getting this product out and while we're talking about it, we may have to go to some of these other niggas and see if they are willing to switch sides and do business with us," he said.

"What we're not trying to do is start another war while we're knee deep in one already. We will deal with Sam for now and others will fall in line. Trust me, bro," I said as I hopped off the expressway on Pulaski and headed to Big Jim's trap on 26th Street.

Slim was usually around this way but I didn't know if I would find him since we basically shut Floyd's ass down. Riding slowly down the block, there were a couple kids outside but that was about it. Bending the corner, I went back around the block and low and behold, Slim was coming out of the corner store. He had his head down trying to open a bag of chips, but was having the hardest time.

Beep! Beep! Beep!

I honked my horn to get his attention and he stopped mid stride and looked up. "Aye yo, Slim!" I hollered out the window. "Come take a ride with me."

"Reese is that you, man? Oh, shit my nigga back," he said dropping his chips running to the car. When he got closer, he paused for a minute and scratched his head. Slim was higher than a muthafucka. "How the fuck you still look young as hell and I'm looking like this?" He asked sadly.

"I'm not Reese, Slim. It's me, Ricio."

"Ricio, man you had a nigga all happy for nothing shit. I thought my nigga was back and I dropped my damn chips," he said looking back at the chips on the ground. He turned to go get them but I wasn't about to let him do that shit. I checked my surrounding before opening the door and got out.

"Put those down, Slim and get in the car. I'll get you something to eat, fam."

Knocking the chips out of his hand, I led him back to my ride. Slim was dirty as hell and he smelled like rotten eggs. I felt bad for him because I'd never seen him in this state before. Yeah, he got high, but this was the worse I'd ever witnessed him being.

Slim got in the backseat and I jumped in the front. Rodrigo let the window down as soon as I closed the door and looked at me evilly. It wasn't my muthafuckin' fault and I didn't care about the smell. I found who I was looking for.

"Ricio, you got something I can hold until I go do this job in a couple days? You know I'm good for it, I'll pay you back."

"Slim, we are about to grab some food and then I'm gon' take you to a hotel so you can take a bath. We'll talk about that other shit later. You already look like you've had enough for now anyway. Is that cool with you?" I asked trying to reason with him.

"I need something to hold me over. I'm not high enough to be alright." Hearing him say that shit shocked the hell out of me because the nigga was higher than a kite.

"Sit back and enjoy the ride, nigga. The man just told you what the plan was. There won't be no negotiating around this muthafucka. He didn't outright say it to you, but I will. You ain't getting shit!" Rodrigo said turning to look Slim in the eye. "Deal with that monkey jumping all over yo' back until we get where we going."

"Aight, Youngblood, I hear you. I'm gon' sit my black ass back because word on the street is, yo' ass crazy."

I saw Rodrigo about to react and grabbed him just in time. "Turn yo' ass around and let that shit go. You act like he lying," I said laughing.

"Fuck you, brah. Hurry the fuck up because this nigga stank. Where the fuck you getting something to eat from? It gotta be something quick. Matter fact, hit Jew Town, we can get some polishes and cheeseburgers with some fries. I ain't had one of them in a good minute."

I was back on the expressway heading toward Roosevelt when Rodrigo's phone rang. He answered it quickly looking out the window. "Yo, what up?" he said when the call connected. Rodrigo was hanging on to every word the person on the other end was saying.

"Trail his ass everywhere he goes. Call Face or Felon so they can have your back, I don't want you out and about solo. These niggas been too fuckin' quiet," he said. "Okay, I bet he's heading to the hospital. No, it's too much heat to be gunnin' for him right now. Stay on his ass and find out whatever you can on that nigga Shake if that's where he's going.

You gon' have to finesse one of them hoe ass nurses. Shit pay a CNA bitch if you have to but we need that information. Call one of the homies for reinforcement, AK. Don't try to be the fuckin' hero, this ain't the time for that shit, be invisible! Aight, hit me back and let me know you good, bet," he said ending the call.

I glanced in his direction and he was still looking out the window. "What's going on?"

"AK saw Floyd driving down 87th and started following him. He was ready to make Precious twerk but I told him no. If I can't kill, ain't nobody killing. Fuck he thought," Rodrigo said as we pulled up to the polish stand.

He jumped out before I could stop the car completely and walked to the counter. I glanced in the rearview mirror and Slim was sleeping like he hadn't slept in days. I felt bad for the cat because he was out there bad. It was going to be a task trying to clean his ass up.

***

After getting something to eat, I went to the Amber Inn on 39th & Michigan to get a room. There was no way I was taking a junkie to my shit to detox. I would have to fuck Slim's ass up if he touched any muthafuckin' thing that didn't belong to him.

"What the fuck we doing here, brah?" Rodrigo asked looking at me crazy.

"I'm about to get a room so this nigga can dry out. I need him to talk to me and he can't do that shit high."

"Man, fuck that, you could've dropped me off at my ride! I'm not about to be babysitting this nigga while he shitting and puking all over the place. He already stank."

"Brah, he's sleep not dead, he might hear you and want to bounce."

"I don't give a fuck! Let me get a ride because you on some bullshit. I could be rollin' with AK gettin' my body count up, you got me fucked up, fam," Rodrigo fumed pulling out his phone. He found the contact he was searching for and put the phone on speaker and a female answered. "Aye, come get me at the Amber Inn on 39th, I need you to take me to my car."

"What the hell you doing over there?"

"Yo' goofy ass man over here and I'm ready to go but he got business to take care of."

"Humph, I don't have a man and me and Kimmie on our way. We're not too far away from there," Nija said hanging up.

I side eyed his ass for a second and went in, "why would you tell her the shit like that, brah? You made it sound like a nigga was trickin' off!"

"Nigga calm yo' ass down. Maybe now you'll do right by her before you lose her altogether. She's only gonna be dickmatized for so long, actually the way I see it, that shits wearing off quickly," he laughed.

"I don't see shit funny. You foul, nigga," I said getting out of the car to pay for the room. I marched to the office and a fine ass female was behind the counter. She looked up from the book she was reading and smiled.

"What can I help you with?" she asked licking her lips.

Baby girl stood about 5'4, I would say she was about a hundred fifty pounds, and she was a red bone, just how I liked them. She had a scar running down the side of her face but it didn't do anything but enhanced her beauty in my eyes. Her hair was bone straight with a part down the middle and flowed down her back.

Licking my lips, I leaned on the counter. "First you can give me your number, then I need a room for a couple nights, Brittany," I responded smoothly reading her nametag.

"How you want my number but you about to lay up? Niggas ain't shit," she said typing away on the keyboard in front of her.

"When you assume, you make an ass out of yourself, ma. I'm about to chill, ain't no female even with me. Don't speak prematurely if you don't know what's going on. Now, write your number down and stop being so mean." I smirked.

"That's game but I'm good on that. What's your definition of a couple nights?" she asked getting back to business.

"Give me the room for a week. I wanna be around to see your face for a while. That would give me time to get your number and maybe take you out. What's the damage?" I asked.

"Seven days would be," she said tallying up my total. "Six hundred sixty-eight dollars. I'll need your license as well."

Pulling a knot of cash from my pocket, I counted out a G and handed it to her along with my ID. "Keep the change and do something nice for yourself, beautiful."

Her eyes lit up when she saw the money. She put my information in the computer and turned to retrieve the key. Scribbling on a piece of paper, she gave me back my ID with the paper attached. "Enjoy your stay, Mr. Vasquez," she smiled.

"Thank you. I'll see you around, Shawty."

I left with a smile on my face because she tried to be tough but money makes a bitch change their mind quick. I'll have her ass bent over sooner than she thinks. The smile vanished when I saw Nija's car parked next to mine. She was looking directly at me and didn't move an inch. The shit had me hotter than a muthafucka. I strolled over to her opened window and stared down on her.

"How you doing, beautiful?"

"Is that the same thing you were saying to the bitch at the counter in there?" she asked pointing toward the hotel office.

"I went in there to get the keys to my room. Don't start this shit, Nija." I said annoyed.

"It doesn't matter, Ricio. I just came to get bro, so I can go about my day. Continue to do you, boo and I'll do the same."

"What the fuck that suppose to mean? You gon' do you?" I growled.

"Just what I said. Take it however you want to take it, Ricio. I'm not about to argue with you about anything. We still cool, let's not take it to a level where I'll stop fucking with you altogether. We will never be enemies, just not an item. Rodrigo, Kimmie, let's go!" She yelled.

"Aight, Ni, be careful out here. I still got my eyes on you," I said nodding my head at her.

"I'll catch up with you later bro and good luck with that nigga. His ass is still knocked out so you may be carrying him inside like a baby," Rodrigo said patting me on the back.

"Shid, that nigga gon' wake the fuck up and walk. The only muthafucka I'm carrying anywhere is my wife as I crossover the threshold on our wedding day," I replied staring at the side of Nija's face. "But hit me up if anything goes down. Stop by the crib and scoop up cuz and nem. Get them niggas out for a minute."

"I can do that. I'm out. Kimmie get yo' fine ass in the backseat, I only roll shotgun baby. We can share that seat if you riding on my lap though," he grinned.

Kimmie rolled her eyes and got in the back seat without acknowledging what Rodrigo said. The way bro was watching her ass, it was a matter of time before he would try to smash. But Kimmie wasn't one of these hoes that he was used to, she was on a whole other level.

Watching as Nija backed the car out of the parking spot, I wanted to ask her to stay with me. Instead I hollered, "I love you, Nija!" She held her arm out the window and stuck up her middle finger. I treaded over to my ride and jumped in. The room was on the other end of the parking lot, I wanted to be close as possible so Slim could walk in on his own.

I hopped out the car and opened the back door. "Aye yo' Slim!" I said shaking his shoulder. "Get up, nigga and get out!"

"Huh? Where the fuck we at Reese?" he asked groggily.

"We at a motel and I told you before, I'm Ricio. Reese is gone, man."

"Why we here?" he asked skeptically.

"I told you I wanted to holla at you and I know you don't have nowhere else to go. You need to get a good night's sleep, now get out."

"You gon' give me some blow when we get in there?" he asked.

"Yeah, I got you," I lied to get his hype ass out my shit. Little did he know his ass was about to experience the worst days of his life getting that toxic shit out his system. He was going to be mad at me but he would thank me later for saving his life.

Slim jumped out quick as hell and waited for me to lead him to the room. I felt sorry for lying to him because he was eager to get inside to get a hit. Walking along the doors I kept my eyes on the numbers until I saw room 106 and inserted the key. Slim damn near pushed me out of the way to get inside. Closing the door and locking it, I went to a chair and sat down.

"Let me get that from you, Youngin. A nigga is feeling kind of sick right now," Slim said pacing back and forth.

I held my head down holding my breath because I was getting pissed because his mind was on crack and nothing else. Slowly I let the air out of my lungs and squinted my eyes at this nigga but he was too busy geeking to notice.

"Slim, I'm gon' be honest with you, I don't have any drugs on me. The reason you're here is because my father told me to find you and help you get clean. When Reese speaks, I respond and this is something he wanted me to do."

"Reese is gone, those are the words that came out of your mouth. What type of fuckin' games are you playing, Ricio? This shit is not funny. I'm sick man and I need drugs!" Slim screamed with his fist balled up at his sides. "Why the fuck did you bring me here?"

"I already told you I brought you here to help you, Slim—"

"Fuck that shit! Ain't nobody tried to help me in years! When your daddy was alive, he was the only one that looked out for me. Reese made sure I had clothes, drugs, food, and a place to lay my head. After he was killed, I didn't have shit!" he cried as he punched the wall. I let him vent because deep down I knew forcing him to detox was scary for him.

"I'm not my daddy but I will help you anyway I can, starting with getting the drugs out yo' system. You will be straight on clothes, food, and shelter, but I will never give you drugs. Slim you are going to hate me for the next seven days or however long it takes," I explained. "You're mad and I understand, but you will not be leaving this room. We can tear this muthafucka up if that's what you need to do, but I have to do what I brought you here for."

Slim plopped down on the bed holding his head in his hands. Sweat covered the top of his head and his left leg bounced vigorously with every grunt that came from his mouth. I got up from the chair and went to the door and left. Coming back with the bags of food in my hand, I sat one down on the bed beside him.

"Eat, Slim. It may make you feel better," I said sitting back in the chair opening my own bag.

Lifting his head, Slim grabbed the bag and inspected the contents inside. He pulled out a polish with fries and took a huge bite. The two of us sat quietly for a few minutes before I decided to break the silence.

"Slim, tell me what you know about Big Jim and Floyd."

The polish he had was no more. Slim reached inside the bag and brought out a burger and a bottle of pop. Unwrapping the sandwich, he took a hefty bite and unscrewed the cap on his pop taking a long swig. Holding the bottle between his legs, Slim continued to eat.

Clearing his throat, Slim finally was ready to talk. His demeanor was calmer and his belly was full. "What I know about them muthafuckas is they had something to do with Reese getting killed and the lil homie Max too. I told Reese about some shit I heard days before his death and he kind of blew the shit off. For years I've blamed myself because I should've tried harder to get him to listen to me."

"What was you trying to get him to listen to?" I asked curiously.

"One day I was on the block just hanging around hoping somebody would feel sorry for me and give me a rock. Big Jim pulled up in his Escalade and I knew he would be my ticket to get high." Slim zoned out reliving the day he spoke on. "I walked up to him and asked if I could wash his truck for rocks. He agreed before calling Floyd over to where he was getting the cleaning supplies out of the back of his ride.

I leaned on the side waiting when I heard Big Jim tell him that it was time to get rid of Reese. My ears perked up and I took in everything that was said that day. They were going over different scenarios of how they would kill him. Hearing them plotting on the one person that looked out for me was a shot to my heart. I knew I had to tell him what was up," he said taking a sip from the bottle.

"I washed Big Jim's truck that day with a lot of shit on my mind, including getting high. Reese came around the next day and I didn't hesitate telling him what Big Jim was planning. He kind of laughed it off and told me don't worry about it because they weren't gon' do shit. Three days later, he was dead. I need a hit in order to continue," he blurted out.

"You tried it, Slim. I'm not giving you no drugs," I laughed. "We don't have nothing but time. You don't have to talk no more right now, I know for sure there's more that you know and you will reveal it. I'm a patient muthafucka," I smirked at him.

Meesha

Chapter 12
Nihiyah

I dug a hole that was hard for me to get out of. Agreeing to set my sister up so Floyd could get to Ricio was a bit extreme, but Nija worsened the blow when she chose to go against the grain. The only thing I wanted was a couple dollars and the bitch turned her nose up at me like I was scum on her shower walls. It shouldn't have mattered what I was using the money for, she was going to get the shit back. Maybe not, but it sounded good.

Nija was the least of my worries. Floyd was expecting her head on a platter because his homie was missing. And he wanted me to deliver her to him. When he rolled up on me, I won't lie I was scared shitless. He jumped out of the car and I wanted to run but I knew he would've shot my ass in the back.

With Shake being in the hospital, I had no one to protect me other than my mama. There was no other choice but to tell her what I had gotten myself into. She was going to be mad but I had to come clean to somebody because Ricio was going to kill my ass if he found out it was me that was feeding Floyd information. I was ready to tell the truth and face the consequences.

Getting behind the wheel of my car, I drove slowly down Madison Street and saw my girl Jolie walking toward one of our get high spots. I knew I should've kept going to my mama's house, but the thought of getting high took over. "Aye, bitch! Where you off to?" I asked riding alongside her like I didn't already know.

"Hey Hiyah! To the spot, you wanna roll?"

"Hell yeah, I don't have shit on me though."

"Girl bye, you know I got you," she said snatching the passenger side door open and hopping in before I could stop the car. "There's enough for both of us. We about to get high as fuck!"

Jolie wasn't lying, she had more than enough crack. She had hit one of the dope boy's stash and ran off. It didn't matter how she got it. I was smoking. An hour later I could barely see as I took Jolie to her house. Driving very cautiously, I made it to my destination in one piece.

I sat in the car for about thirty minutes before I started the journey to my mama's house. My vision was hazy and it was nothing but God that I made it safely without causing an accident. I saw Nija's car parked in the driveway and my first thought was to just leave. Instead, I parked beside her car and got out.

As I opened the door to enter the house, the scent of my mama's homemade meatballs filled my nostrils. The last thing I ate was a bag of barbeque chips that I stole from a gas station the day before. My stomach growled loudly and I couldn't wait to fix me a plate. Nija's voice filled my ears and she was running her mouth to my mama about what happened at her job. The thought of food was a thing of the past as I listened to her whine.

"She had no reason to be coming to my job with her crap. Then she got mad because I wouldn't give her my hard earned money. Your daughter has a problem and she need help, ma. Nihiyah's body odor was disgusting! Oh my God!

She embarrassed the hell out of me and even spit in my food. I wanted to beat her ass but my stomach was hurting from me throwing up because her breath smelled so bad. My boss suspended me until Monday so, not only did she cause a scene, I'm losing money behind her retarded ass."

"Wait a minute, she came to your job acting a plum fool?"

"Yes, ma. All because I wouldn't give her money. Hiyah is out there bad and she needs help. The way she was showing out, she was definitely tweaking."

Appearing in the entryway of the living room, I snarled at Nija as she told my mama everything. It wasn't her place to disclose anything about me to anyone, especially not my mama. The whole point of me coming there was to talk her about what I was going through. But of course, Miss Goody two shoes came crying for sympathy.

"You talk too fuckin' much, bitch! Shit like this is the reason I used to fuck you up when we were growing up!" I spat at my sister.

"Nihiyah Foster! Watch your mouth in my house, girl. What the hell is your problem?" my mama asked standing from the couch.

"I don't have a problem but that bitch about to have one," I rushed toward Nija with my fist clenched to my sides and my mother stepped in front of me. "Move out of my way!"

"Who the fuck you think you're screaming at? Stop this bullshit because there will be no fighting in here today! When was the last time you brushed your teeth or took a bath for that matter, Hiyah? I have never seen you walking around like this."

"Don't try to twist things around on me—"

"This entire conversation was about you, what do you mean? That's why you're so upset. I want you to answer one question and honestly. Are you on drugs?" my mama asked with a hurt look on her face.

"I smoke weed every now and again," I said downplaying my situation.

"Weed ain't never had nobody walking around dirty and stankin'. You need to tell the truth so we can get you some help, Nihiyah," Nija said putting in her two cents.

"Get me help? Bitch you wouldn't even give me a couple dollars but you want to pay for treatment, miss me with that bullshit!"

"I will never give you money to smoke that shit and I'm not talking about weed either," Nija rolled her eyes and folded her arms over her chest. "The way you acted up at my job and how dirty you are today, you on crack! Own up to it!"

"So what I smoke crack every once in a while, that don't mean I got a problem!"

"You sound dumb as fuck, don't tell nobody else that shit because they'll laugh in your face."

"Nija, be quiet for a damn minute!" my mama screamed with tears in her eyes. She turned to me and I knew I had disappointed her in a way I'd never done before. "Why, Hiyah. What could be so wrong in your life that you turned to drugs? Wasn't I a good mother to you?"

Aht, Aht mama, don't you blame yourself for the way she decided to live her life. This is all on her, not you," Nija interjected.

"It's not your fault that I'm the way I am. I haven't been the same since daddy up and left us in the cold. Getting over that hurt was something I was never able to do. I started smoking weed when I was sixteen years old and you didn't even know about it. Sex was my recreational activity back then when you thought I was out being a sweet high school kid.

I was out looking for the father figure that walked out on us. I was doing fine until this bitch, started thinking she was better than me," I said pointing at Nija. "While I was getting played by every nigga that crossed my path, she had Ricio to cater to her spoiled ass. Not only did I come second to her at home, I came second to her in the streets too."

"Get that sorry ass sob story out of here, Nihiyah. My relationship with Ricio didn't have shit to do with you smoking crack! Tell that shit to somebody else. You did that shit because that's what you wanted to do, admit it and stop trying to blame everybody else!" Nija screamed.

"Calm down, Nija. Nihiyah, if this was bothering you so much you should've come to me. We could've talked about your feelings and gotten your father involved so you could've told him how you felt. Drugs is not the way to handle that hurt. It has only put you in a position to mess up your life."

"My life was ruined when he walked out on us and we had to move! Do you know how many times I've called him and he told me he would call me back? Plenty of times and I'm still waiting on his ass to call years later," I cried.

"I will get you the help that you need, baby," my mama said walking toward me.

"I don't need help," I said wiping my hand down my face.

"It's either you accept the help I'm offering or you will have to leave my house. I won't allow you to be using drugs under my roof or even coming in high as a kite. Your choice, Nihiyah."

"You putting me out?" I asked astonished. "Where will I go, huh?" One minute you want to help me with a problem I don't have, then give me an ultimatum the next. Who does that?"

"I do, dammit! I won't sit back and watch you destroy your life. I put in blood, sweat, and tears to make sure both of you were well taken care of. But lately there has been so much bullshit happening that I don't understand where I went wrong," my mama sobbed.

I didn't like to see my mama cry but there was nothing I could do to console her. I told her that I used but it wasn't enough to get her off my back. She was hurt I understood that, but I wasn't the only child of hers that was making noise in the street. It was time for me to blow up my sister's spot.

"While you're jumping on me about what I'm doing, how about you ask your daughter about the shit she's into behind a nigga! There are people out to kill her ass because of Ricio but you focusing on me and what I'm doing."

"I didn't want to believe that you were the one behind the shit that happened to me. Thanks for confirming what I should've never doubted. How could you put me in the line of fire for drugs, Nihiyah? You're my sister and you sold your soul to the devil for drugs! You fed those men information about me so they could come after me! You dirty bitch! I could've died because of you!" Nija yelled charging at me. My mama once again intervened preventing her from getting close to me.

"What are you talking about, Nija?" my mama asked struggling to keep her away from me.

"The same day her dope fiend ass came to my job, a dude followed me from 83rd all the way to Harvey. It didn't dawn on me that my sister was the one that led this nigga to me. I had to call Rodrigo to save me and I do believe that man would've killed me if I hadn't. Fuck you Nihiyah! From this point on I don't give a fuck what happens to you! Stay the fuck away from me!"

"Nihiyah, are you out there telling people where to find your sister?"

"Why would I want somebody to hurt my own flesh and blood? I didn't tell nobody—"

Nija broke away from my mother's grip and swung her fist hitting me dead in the mouth. Stumbling back, I didn't see the next

115

blow coming until it was too late. I saw a flash of light and my eye felt like it had been pushed to the back of my head.

"Stop, Nija!" mama screamed as she pulled her off me.

"You a muthafuckin' lie! The dude that was following me said he was told where I worked and he pulled a fuckin' gun on me! I could've died because of her hype ass! You're dead to me, hoe. There's no way to fix this shit. Mama I'm sorry, but I gotta go. I love you and I'll call you later," Nija said walking toward me.

I moved to the other side of the room just in case she wanted to swing again but, she only snatched the door open and left. Staring back at the door as if she would come back, my mama was shooting daggers at me as tears fell down her face. She shook her finger at me for a few seconds while shaking her head.

"If I find out you did what Nija said you did, I'm gonna press charges on your ass myself. I'm telling you now, if anything happens to my baby, I'll be the one going to jail for killing my own daughter. Go upstairs, pack your shit and get the fuck out of my house. I was serious when I said wasn't no drugs or addicts living up in here. Nihiyah, you won't get one chance to steal from me.

You better hope you can get out of this mess because if they kill you, all I can say is your insurance is paid. You went against family. The very person that has been there for you whenever you fucked up. Get out of my face and go pack your shit. While you're at it, wash your stankin' ass and brush your damn teeth. Out here running around like don't nobody give two hells about your ass.

You look pathetic and I only wanted you to tell me the truth, anyone that can see and the ones that can't, could tell you smoking. You got thirty minutes to do what you gotta do before I call the police." I couldn't believe my mama was treating me this way. She had never taken sides when me and Nija got into an altercation. "What the fuck are you still standing there for? Go before I change my mind and make you leave with nothing!" my mama shouted.

At that point, I knew she was beyond pissed, but she chose the wrong side to be on. I had something for her backstabbing ass too.

Chapter 13
Nija

I had to get out of that house before I choked the fuck out of Nihiyah. It pained me to hear her speak on someone trying to kill me because the only way for her to know was if she was involved. Her knowledge of what happened had me thinking about what else had she told them. If she died, she deserved however she went out. When I got in my car, I called Kimmie but her phone went straight to voicemail. I tried a second time and she answered right before the voicemail would've picked up.

"Hey Nija, what's up boo?" she asked.

"Are you at home?"

"Yeah, I'm here. What's wrong?"

"I'll explain when I get there. Open the garage for me, I'm on my way. Leaving my mama's house," I said ending the call.

It took less than three minutes to get to Kimmie's house and I was glad because the tears that clouded my vision wouldn't allow me to go any further. As soon as I turned into the driveway, the door to the garage opened and I pulled inside. As I was getting out of my car, I could've sworn I saw Nihiyah's car speed past. The last thing I needed was for her to see me at Kimmie's house.

Walking to the door that led to the kitchen, I hit the button to let the garage door down and went inside. My best friend was standing at the stove stirring some damn noodles and my mouth started watering thinking about the meatballs with gravy, mash potatoes, and corn that I left back at my mama's house.

"When are you gonna stop eating that bullshit?" I asked sitting at the glass table.

"Shit, I haven't had the chance to go to the grocery store and I don't have to cook, I'm the only bitch living in this damn house. My bad, I forgot you live here temporarily now. I still cook when I feel like it," she laughed as she added a little margarine to the small pot. "You've been crying, talk to me. What's going on?" she asked glancing in my direction.

Holding my head in my hands, I fought hard not to cry but it wasn't working. Kimmie brought two bowls of noodles to the table and placed on in front of me. I had no plans of eating any of it and pushed the bowl away. The aroma alone was making my stomach churn.

"The other day Nihiyah came to my job asking for money. When I told her no, she started going ballistic and got me suspended from work. I left a few minutes after she was escorted out and I was followed until I got on the expressway. Once I noticed the same car was behind me the entire way, I called Rodrigo to tell him what I suspected. He gave instructions to lead the dude to a remote area.

Rodrigo ended up killing him but before he did, the guy told him that a crackhead female told him where to find me. I didn't put two and two together until Nihiyah mentioned something about me getting killed behind Ricio. No one knew about what happened with the guy except me, Rodrigo and whoever sent the guy to kill me," I explained.

"How did you figure he would kill you? And why am I just hearing about this? You came to stay with me on Thursday," Kimmie said letting her fork fall into the bowl.

"He pulled a muthafuckin' gun out and shot at the window! It was a good thing Rodrigo told me to get out of my car and run to his as soon as I got to the spot. If I had stayed in my car, I would've died. Rodrigo's car is bulletproof and saved my life. I didn't tell you because I didn't want you to worry."

"That's fucked up! I told you Nihiyah was on that shit and would do anything to get high. It doesn't surprise me that she threw you in the line of fire for a couple seconds of buzz. You should've whooped her ass," Kimmie said scooping up a forkful of noodles.

"Oh, I did get a few hits on her ass before my mama stopped me. If had a gun I would've shot her ass. Shit, she's killing herself slowly anyway. May as well put her stupid ass out of her misery. Floyd don't give a damn about her. He's going to kill her anyway once he's done with her."

"I hate to say it but I think you're right about that. Eat your food and don't keep shit like that from me again, Ni."

"Kimmie, I'm not eating that shit and you shouldn't either," I said as my phone started ringing in my purse. I looked at the screen and it was my mama. "Yeah, ma."

"Where are you, Nija?"

"I'm at Kimmie's. Are you alright?" I asked worriedly.

"Yeah, I'm okay. I put your sister out. Be careful out there, baby. Your sister is not the same person I raised. I couldn't begin to tell you who that monster is. I'm getting my locks changed tomorrow because I don't trust her. Are you staying with Kimmie tonight? I don't think you should go home tonight."

"Ma, I haven't been home in the past couple weeks. I was staying with Ricio but I'm good on him right now. I've been staying with Kimmie so, this is where I'll be. Don't worry, Nihiyah ain't that stupid to do anything crazy."

"I'm packing up half of this food so you can eat. Come back over and get it," she said as I heard her tearing aluminum foil from the roll.

"Ma, I don't feel like going back out. I'll send Kimmie to get the food because I'm hungry. She's in here trying to make me eat some Raman noodles," I said disgustedly.

"Kimmie knows better than that. As a matter fact, I'm sending all the food over. I have a plate up for myself. I'll be waiting for her to pull up. I love you, Nija. Call me and let me know that you are alright every day."

"I will mama, I love you too," I said ending the call. "Bestie, go over to mama's and get the food she packed up for us please. I'm tired."

"What did she cook?" she asked eating another forkful of noodles.

"Meatballs, mashed potatoes, and corn."

Kimmie was out of her seat putting her shoes on the minute I said meatballs. She didn't play when it came down to my mama's cooking. "You don't' have to tell me twice, I'll be right back. Fuck those noodles."

I laughed for the first time within the hour because Kimmie was a fool. Sitting staring at my phone, I contemplated calling Ricio but

I didn't want to talk to him at all. Instead, I went to the living room and kicked off my shoes and laid across the couch. Picking up the remote I turned the tv on and there was a breaking news report. I hadn't missed much so I tuned in to see what was going on.

Reporting from the forest preserve on 147th & Loomis in Harvey, the body of an African American male has been discovered in a dumpster. He has several gunshot wounds and was pronounced dead on the scene. There are no other details about the murder but if anyone have any information, please contact Crime Stoppers at the number displayed below. Stay tuned for more on the ten o'clock news. This is Gabrielle Sanchez signing off.

Immediately getting nervous, I grabbed my phone and called Rodrigo. "What up, sis," he said when he answered.

"Did you see the news? They found—"

"Yo' don't talk about that shit over the phone! Where you at?" he asked.

"I'm at Kimmie's house."

"I'll be there in a minute. She still in the same spot not too far from yo' mama, right?"

"Yeah she's still there."

"Bet, see you in about an hour, sis. Don't worry about nothing, we good," he said disconnecting the call.

As soon as I placed my phone on the coffee table, Kimmie walked back into the house balancing a pan and two bowls in her right arm. I got up and took the bowls from her and walked into the kitchen. I didn't wait for her to put the pan down before I snatched a plate from the cabinet and washed my hands. I put four meatballs on the plate along with some mash potatoes and corn. Covering the plate with a napkin, I threw it in the microwave for two minutes.

"Kimmie they found the body of the guy that followed me Thursday. I called Rodrigo because that shit scared the shit out of me. He will be here in a little while. He didn't want to talk about it over the phone."

"Good for his slimy ass. I wish they would've never found his bitch ass. He came for the wrong muthafucka," she said making her a plate.

I stood staring at her because she was fixing a plate like she hadn't eaten all day and I'd sat watching her inhale half of those nasty ass noodles. "You're not going to eat all that damn food, Kimmie. You just finished eating before you left. It didn't take long for you to go get the food from mama."

"Bitch, the noodles were an appetizer. This right here, nigga, is the main course," she said laughing. I'm about to fuck this shit up!" she said as the microwave timer started beeping.

Sitting at the table with my plate in hand, I cut a piece of meatball and shoved it in my mouth. The minute I tried to swallow, I felt it coming back up. Jumping up from the table, I ran down the hall to the bathroom retching barely making it to the toilet

Vomit spewed from my mouth splashing the water back onto my face. It disgusted me and made me puke more. Hearing footsteps behind me, I knew Kimmie was there to make sure I was alright.

"Nija, are you good?"

Spitting in the toilet, I turned and nodded my head up and down. "I'm good," I said dry heaving. "I don't think my stomach agreed with the meatballs my mama made."

"Since when? You love mama Pat's meatballs. There has to be more to what's going on," Kimmie said leaning against the door frame.

"It has to be—" Before I could finish what I was saying, a rush of bile forced its way up my throat and out my mouth.

"Ewww! Damn Nija, I think I saw a lung come out of your mouth. Hold up, I know what the fuck is wrong with yo' ass. Keep throwing up, get it all out because we are about to do an experiment on your ass," Kimmie said leaving me there to die alone.

After a few minutes of waiting, my stomach stopped churning. I stood to my feet and flushed the toilet and turned the water on in the sink. Lathering soap on my hand, I washed my face and snatched my toothbrush from the holder. While brushing, Kimmie appeared in the doorway with a smirk on her face.

"You good now?" she asked.

"Yeah," I replied spitting in the sink. "I'm alright and hungry as hell."

Rinsing my mouth in the sink, I grabbed a towel from the rack and wiped my face. When I looked in the mirror, Kimmie was standing waving an object in the air. I turned around and she was smiling while tearing open a damn pregnancy test.

"What the hell you doing with that?" I asked confused. "I know damn well you don't think I'm pregnant."

"That's exactly what I think, bitch. We're about to take this test and if it's not positive, then to the emergency room we go. But my mind is telling me what I already know. You and the man you are so in love with are about to be parents," Kimmie said holding out the test for me to take.

"You should've saved this for your own ass, it's about to be a waste of a good test. I'm not pregnant! The only reason I'm taking it is to prove your ass wrong." I snatched the test from her with confidence and rolled it between my fingers waiting for her to leave. "Get out, Kimmie! I'm not taking a drug test in this muthafucka. I know how to piss on a stick."

"Hurry up and leave it sitting on the sink for both of us to see the results together," she said slamming the bathroom door.

Staring at the test for a minute, I thought back to the last time I had my period. It was hard to remember but I was sure I had one last month. I was surely going to check my app that I used to track that hoe once I pissed on this stick. As I sat down on the commode, it didn't take long for a stream of urine to flow. I stuck the tip of the test in the stream, getting it nice and wet and put the cap back on, sitting it on the counter.

After wiping myself, I washed my hands and left the test there to do whatever it was created to do. Kimmie was sitting at the table and she had warmed up my food again for me. I sat down and tried to eat once again because I was hungry. The second time around it was good as hell. Kimmie sat back without saying anything but she kept checking the time on her phone.

The results of that damn test meant more to her than it did me because I knew what they were. It would be a cold day in hell before I pushed out a baby and it wasn't going to be by Mauricio Vasquez.

Standing to wash my plate, Kimmie grabbed my arm and pulled me away from the table.

"That can wait, we need to go see what this test is talking about."

"Nawl, man that shit can wait. I already know what it'll say. I'm not in a rush to see the negative results that's going to be displayed in the window. As a matter of fact," I said snatching away from her. "I'll prove that I had a menstrual last month."

"Nija, that don't mean nothing at all. Save that bullshit for somebody that don't know any better. The test will tell all." She left me going through my app and went to the bathroom. "Just like I thought! Bitch you pregnant than a muthafucka but you're in denial," Kimmie said running out of the bathroom waving the test around.

"I'm gon' be an auntie! I'm gon' be an auntie!"

"What? You lying, Kimmie, stop playing with me," I said seriously. "This is not the time to be pulling pranks."

"Ain't no pranks today, you about to be a mommy! You about to be a mommy, I'm about to be an auntie!" Kimmie sang loudly as she danced around the room.

I was not participating in her happy dance because I was far from happy. There was no way I was pregnant and she had yet to show me the test. In my mind, she was telling a damn lie.

"Let me see for myself because yo' ass is always trying to be funny."

"Here you go, take a look. Two lines means pregnant. Boom, bitch! I'm about to be an auntie! I'm about to be an auntie!" she started singing again.

Ding Dong

The doorbell rang but I was stuck in the middle of the room and couldn't move as I looked at the proof of the test. Rodrigo's voice made me instantly stuff the test in my back pocket and I turned to face the door as he and another guy walked into the house.

"Why the hell you doing all that hollering Kimmie? And who about to be an auntie?" he asked looking back and forth between Kimmie and I.

"Nobody is about to be anything. You know Kimmie is always playing childish ass games, bro."

"Nija, don't lie. I've been standing outside that door for a good five minutes and I heard her say that you were also about to be a mommy. Now, I'm gon' ask one time, are you pregnant?" Rodrigo asked with his eyebrow raised.

"According to the test yes, but I will be going to the doctor first thing Monday to find out for sure. Please don't tell your brother, Rodrigo.

"You got me fucked up, Nija. I won't keep no shit like that from him. What ya'll got going on to warrant him not knowing about his seed? he asked pulling his phone out.

I knew then Rodrigo was about to hurt his brother's feelings by telling him I was pregnant. This baby wasn't going to see the light of day if I had anything to do with it.

Chapter 14
Ricio

Slim was sleeping like he hadn't slept comfortably in a very long time. We had a few hurdles to cross the first couple hours because he was craving a hit and his ass didn't understand that he was not getting shit. I had to beat his ass softly, I didn't want to hurt him. But he was sporting a few bumps and bruises. That was the reason he was sleeping like a baby. My phone vibrated on the dresser and I reached over without looking at it and answered.

"Talk to me."

"Yo, Ricio, I have a little bit of news for you about Floyd. He has setup shop on the Southside and has a whole army of niggas riding with him. I guess since we took all his hittas from him on the westside, he's using the ones out south.

There's a trap on 76th and Sangamon, 63rd and Loomis, 76th and Damen, and the last one on 75th and Calumet. When I tell you, this nigga got some heavy hittas, he got heavy hittas. His money flow hasn't been affected because business is still going strong for him. I think we should take over his spots on the westside then hit them niggas so we can take over the Southside too."

As I listened to AK tell me Floyd was still getting money hand over fist it pissed me off. His ass only moved his shit to the other side of the city and thought I wouldn't find out about it. Floyd must've forgot I had thorough muthafuckas on my team too. It was about time to get some shit in place to take over the city. At first, I was only going to supply weight but fuck that, I wanted it all.

"You followed him for a while without him spotting you?" I asked curiously.

"Ricio, this nigga's mind can't be on the war he has caused with us. He acted like he didn't have a care in the world. Floyd seemed like he never expected you or anyone else to find him on that side of the city. To answer your question, yeah, I followed him to every location. They have heavy artillery and when it comes to sellin' that product, they got it on lock!" AK replied.

We got this fam and thanks for the information. I'm dealing with some shit right now—" I paused as another called came in on my phone. "Hold on, brah, I gotta answer this. Don't hang up," I said clicking over. "What up, brah?"

"Ricio, you need to get to Kimmie's crib right now!" Rodrigo said in a serious tone.

"What's wrong with Kimmie? Wait, is it Nija?"

"Yeah, it's Nija but it's nothing bad so calm down. I just need you to get here because I'm not the one to ever hold anything like this from you. She's pregnant and didn't want me to tell you but she got me fucked up."

"You know I got Slim in this room and I can't just leave. Wait hold on a minute," I said going back to AK. "Aye, AK come to the Amber Inn on 39th Street, Room 106. I need you to sit with this nigga Slim while I go check on Nija."

"Say less, my nigga. I'm on the eway now. I'll be there in about ten minutes. Be ready to roll when I pull up," he said hanging up.

"This nigga got some nerve putting me on hold like I'm some kind of hoe. I just told his jug head ass that Nija is pregnant and he conducting business like I didn't say a damn thing to him," Rodrigo was going on and on talking to himself and didn't realize I was back on the phone.

"Nigga I had to make previsions for somebody to come and sit in this room! I'll be there in thirty, you whinny ass muthafucka!" I said bangin' on his ass.

Slim was still sleeping which was fine by me because his chest was moving so I knew he was alive. I got up from the bed and went to the door and opened it. At that moment, I saw AK's car turn into the motel's parking lot. Looking back into the room, Slim hadn't moved and I was cool with dipping out to handle this situation.

"Hey, fam. Everything cool with Nija?" AK asked as he exited his car.

"Yeah, she's cool. Rodrigo called telling me that she's pregnant and didn't want him to tell me. If that was the case, she shouldn't have told the nigga because she knew he was gon' tell me. Nija's ass is trying to be petty because she ain't fuckin' with me right now. That shit don't have nothing to do with my seed.

Enough about that shit. I want you to go in there and watch Slim. His ass is going through withdrawals and I'm taking him through the process of drying out. Under no circumstance are you to give him any type of drug. I don't give a fuck if he's complaining about a headache, he don't get shit!"

I'll stop and get some food and do a little shopping for him before I come back. I'll hit you up when I'm on my way and don't hesitate to hit me up if something goes down. Just to let you know, his ass may try to fight. Beat his ass if you have to, but he's not to leave this muthafucka."

"I got you and congratulations on your bundle. I've never thought you would slip up and start a family," AK laughed. "Yo' ass don't stay with just one bitch. Nija is a different breed though."

"Thanks, man. I want to be excited too but I can't. I sense bullshit in the making and I don't want to celebrate too early. I'll see you later, watch ya'self," I said walking to my ride.

Driving southbound on the Dan Ryan expressway, I started thinking about the last time I made love to Nija. It was the morning after Max was killed. I could still feel her sugary walls sliding along my joint. The thought alone made me brick up.

All of that went out the window when I turned down the street that Kimmie lived. I started wondering why Nija didn't want me to know about her pregnancy. Giving myself a pep talk as I parked on the street, I cleared my mind and exited my vehicle. Rodrigo opened the door as I walked up the steps and met me halfway.

"What up, bro? How's Slim?" he asked.

"Man, that nigga is going through it. His ass wanted to fight because I wouldn't give him drugs. But I whooped his ass and he laid the fuck down and went to sleep. AK is sitting with him until I handle this situation over here. Tell me what's up before I go in there to talk with Nija."

"I came over because she called saying she heard on the news that the body of the nigga I slumped was found. When I got here, I heard Kimmie singing 'I'm about to be an auntie' over and over.

Then she added you're about to be a mommy. Ringing the doorbell, Kimmie opened it and when I asked who was about to be an auntie, Nija tried to downplay it and say nobody. Then she had the nerve to say not to tell you."

"Say less," I said walking past him into the house. As I entered the living room, Angel and Kimmie was sitting on the couch watching the news. Nija was nowhere to be seen. "What's up cuz? Kimmie where's Nija?" Angel held his fist out for me to dap.

"She is out back in the yard. Ricio, talk to her. Don't go out there trying to preach to her like you're her daddy."

"Man, fuck that shit! There's a reason she didn't want me to know about this pregnancy and I'm about to find out," I said stalking to the back door.

Nija was sitting in a lounge chair when I stepped off the last step. She didn't attempt to look up from her phone and it pissed me off. As I got closer, I noticed the pregnancy test lying on the table beside her and went straight to it. Nija looked up and tried to grab it before I did but she was too slow. I glanced down at the test then at her. She held her head down and started picking at her nails.

"So, you weren't gon' tell me about this, Nija?" I asked calmly.

"To be honest, no. I just learned I was pregnant and haven't processed it myself. Your brother wouldn't even know if it wasn't for Kimmie acting a damn fool after seeing the results. I'm not ready for a baby—"

"Nija, don't play with me! Since the day we started fuckin', all we talked about was having kids together. You ain't ready to have a baby, tell that shit to a nigga that don't know you. I should've been the first person on your line when the test read positive. Stop being petty and grow the fuck up!" I yelled out of frustration because she was pissing me off.

"Grow up? Nigga, please! You got your nerve talking about somebody needing to grow up. I've been grown for a very long time and take care of my responsibilities without help. The help I receive, I have never asked for. The hoes you out here entertaining needs to grow the fuck up while they're riding your dick to make their monthly bill payments.

I refuse to have a baby with you and you're for every bitch that would open their funky ass legs for you. I'm the realest bitch you would ever meet in your fuckin' life! When I said I was done with you, Ricio, I meant that shit. That alone should automatically tell you I won't be having this baby!"

"Nija, you ain't getting rid of my seed, yo'! We would have major muthafuckin' problems if you even tried. Other females are clouding your decision to go through with this pregnancy. I don't know how many times I have to tell you to worry about us! You have my heart. These hoes don't mean shit to me!"

"Obviously I don't, Ricio. You can't keep professing your love for me when you're continuously entertaining other females. I'm not having this baby, period," she stood and walked past me. Before she could get too far, I grabbed her arm and she snatched away from me. "Don't touch me! Leave me the fuck alone, Mauricio!"

Watching her storm back into the house, I looked down at my feet and pinched the bridge of my nose. I had to calm myself before I went into that house and choked the hell out of her. Nija didn't understand the love I had for her didn't need to be explained. But I found myself professing it to her every chance I could but it wasn't enough.

I entered the house and Rodrigo and Angel were sitting on the couch when a breaking news report appeared on the tv. My brother grabbed the remote and turned the volume up. They were reporting from a forest preserve and the police had it surrounded with red tape.

"Reporting from Harvey, a body has been found in a dumpster. The African American male was apparently shot several times. The identity of the victim is being withheld until the family is notified. Police are on the scene collecting evidence that may possibly solve this case. If you have any information about this crime, please call the Harvey Homicide unit at the number below. We will have more updates about this story as they become available. This is Gabrielle Sanchez signing off."

Rodrigo turned the tv down and turned to me. "That's the nigga that was following Nija. Once his name is revealed, Floyd is going to react. It's time to stop sitting around, Ricio. We have to get at these niggas before they attack first."

"I'm with Rodrigo on this one, cuz. Time's being wasted doing nothing. Have y'all heard anything on the nigga that's in the hospital?"

"Nah, I don't know how that nigga doing. Where's Alexander, Javier, Mateo, and Nicolás?

"They were at the hotel last time I talked to Javier. We were thinking about going out but I think we need to get at these fools that's coming for y'all, fam. It's one thing to gun for niggas, but women don't have shit to do with this situation," Angel said seriously.

"You right and to find out Nija is carrying my seed only made matters worse for them. When Floyd finds out his homeboy deader than a doorknob, him and his team are going to go on a rampage. We have to be ready.

AK found out some lucrative information that gave us the upper hand on these niggas. He located the spots they running on the Southside. A meeting is needed to get things moving but I can't get it going until after we meet up with Sam on Monday. Until then, we have to continue to sit tight," I explained.

"You got one day bro, before all hell breaks loose. I've been waiting too long to get at them and you want me to keep sitting on my hands not making a move. That shit ain't gon' happen after today. I'm telling you now, I will be going on a killing spree of my own, with or without y'all," Rodrigo said taking a blunt from behind his ear.

"Bro, on some real shit, I can't stop you from doing what you want to do. You a grown ass man and I'll always be in your corner whenever you need me." I'd tried to keep my brother under control but it was wearing off by the hour. My phone vibrated and Rodrigo's chimed, I snatched mine from my hip and there was a message from Beast.

Beast: Get to my house now!

Rodrigo was on his feet immediately. "Bro, you got that too?" he asked.

"Yeah. We out but I have to holla at Nija first. I'll meet you outside then we can be out," I said walking down the hall to Kimmie's spare bedroom.

"You know where he lives, meet us there because something is wrong," Rodrigo said.

Hearing the door open and close as I walked down the hall, I stood in front of the closed door and twisted the knob. It was locked.

"Ni, open the door, ma."

"Get away from me, Ricio. I don't feel like dealing with your shit."

"Look—never mind. I'll hit you up later so make sure I'm not on the block list. I have something to handle right now," I said turning away. "Kimmie, come lock up, I'm out," I shouted as I left her house.

"All I know is if Nija kills my seed, she better be ready to die right behind it," I thought to myself as I hopped in my ride.

Meesha

Chapter 15
Beast

I was sitting watching tv when a breaking story interrupted the program I was watching. Apparently, a body was found in a dumpster somewhere in Harvey. Listening to the reporter give very little detail about what may have happened, Sin yelled from the laundry room.

"Beast, how many times I have to ask you to check your clothes before you put them in the hamper?" she yelled walking into the living room with something in her hand. "If I hadn't checked your suit jacket, this would've been destroyed. What is it?"

"Hell if I know, give it here," I shot back with my hand out.

When she placed the object in my hand I looked down and it was a disc and my mind drew blank because I didn't know what it was. The news segment had gone off so I got up and walked toward my office to pop the disc into my computer. Sin went back to doing laundry and I was alone to see what I'd forgotten about.

Popping the disc in my Mac, I waited patiently for it to load. I grabbed a Cuban and fired it up to keep me company. The screen displayed a scene of a room that looked like it took place in a police interrogation room. I was confused as hell then Chuck came to mind outside the funeral home the day of Max's service. Suddenly I remembered he'd told me he had something for me to look at as he handed me the disc and I put it in the inside pocket of my suit jacket.

With everything that had taken place that day, the shit skipped my mind. I took a long puff from the cigar before I hit the play button. When I hit play, Max was sitting back in a chair twiddling his thumbs like he was nervous. It seemed like forever before anyone else would enter the room, so I fast forwarded to the part when Big Jim entered.

He walked in with a mean mug on his face until he noticed Max was the one waiting to see him. Then his frown turned to a smile. There was something about how he looked at nephew that rubbed me the wrong way.

"What's up, Maxie?" he asked chuckling as he sat down.

"Don't call me that, Big Jim. I was named Maximo, not Maxie, Stop calling me that shit!"

Max was pissed from what I could see. I would be too. Hell being called Maxie is gay as fuck. I would've punched that nigga in his shit. Tuning back in on what was being said, I prepared myself for whatever was about to happen.

"You didn't seem to mind when I was on the outside. What's the difference now?" he smirked.

"The difference is, you can't act on your sadistic ways in here. I need you to call off Floyd and the rest of the crew. They are talking about killing my brothers and I won't sit back and let that happen."

Max went to the prison that day to try to stop them niggas from moving in on his brother's. Had he told me what he had in mind I would've told him that shit wasn't going to work. Big Jim was a trifling ass nigga that didn't give a fuck about nobody but himself. Rewinding the footage back a bit because I missed Big Jim's response and pressed play once again. He laughed hard as hell at what Max said before he responded.

"What the fuck you mean you won't let it happen? Nigga you ain't got no muthafuckin' say so in the matter! You got the game fucked up! Yo' brother disrespected me after everything I've done for y'all, then he tried to steal my money—"

"Big Jim, Mauricio wasn't stealing from you—"

"If yo' punk ass ever interrupt me when I'm talking again, I will kill you, bitch! Ricio needs to be taught a fuckin' lesson and he is going to get it. I don't know what the fuck you thought coming here was gon' do. I'm not calling off shit! His ass is good as dead, nigga."

"Please, man! Don't do this shit. I don't have nobody left but them, I've already lost my parents, I can't lose them too."

Pressing the pause button, I took a long drag from the cigar and pinched the bridge of my nose. It hurt so bad to see Max begging this pussy ass nigga not to kill his brothers. At the same time, I was pissed because he didn't tell nobody what happened during this damn visit. I opened the bottom drawer of my desk and grabbed the bottle of Remy I kept there for stressful occasions like the one I was enduring. Throwing a couple shots back, I hit the cigar again before taking deep breaths so I could continue watching the footage.

I pressed the play button and stared at the image of Big Jim menacingly. *"What the fuck are you going to do for me to save your brothers? "I haven't felt yo' lips on my dick in a while. Give me that satisfaction right now, and I'll call that shit off today."*

"I'm not doing none of that shit willingly! I didn't enjoy none of what you made me do for years! Why the hell did you do me like that, Big Jim? I need to know! The things you did to me got me out here fucking bitches left and right trying to figure out if I'm actually gay! You molested me, nigga! With a fucking gun to my head every time! Now you want me to sit here and act like I was your boy toy on purpose!"

I heard what Big Jim said but when Max confirmed it with the words he spoke, the ringing in my ears were loud as fuck. I stopped the footage and got up and went upstairs to Sin's stash. The cigar wasn't going to help the way I was feeling at that moment. Taking one of her swisher's and put a nice heaping of weed in a piece of paper, I made my way back downstairs to my office.

Trying to wrap my mind around the shit I'd heard, I wanted to break down and cry. Everything started coming together as to why Max acted the way he did. That faggot ass nigga was fucking that child and again, he didn't say nothing to nobody! Max held that shit in for as long as he could and killed himself thinking the truth would die with him.

Picking up my phone, I sent a text to Ricio and Sosa because the information I had, couldn't be kept secret under any circumstances.

Me: Get to my house now!

Was all I said in the text message I sent to them both. Sin was the last person I wanted to tell what was going on. She was going to explode but I had to tell her. How, was what I had to figure out. Breaking the blunt down, I dumped the contents in the garbage can that sat at my feet.

I tightly rolled the perfect blunt and lit that muthafucka and pulled on it hard. Repeatedly hitting the weed, I let my eyes close to calm my nerves. Sin took that moment to enter my office with her purse hanging from her shoulder.

"Baby, is everything okay?" she asked walking into the room. "What's wrong, Erique?"

Sin knew something had to be wrong for me to be smoking her weed. That was her thing, not mine. As she walked deeper into the room, I reached over and minimized the picture on the computer screen.

"Everything is fine, Sin. Where are you off to?" I asked hitting the blunt again.

"Madysen called and said they're letting her go home. Actually, they discharged her earlier but she claims she was too tired to leave then. I'm on my way to get her and the baby. That can wait though, I'm not leaving until you tell me what's going on."

"I'll fill you in when you get back, Sin. Go get Madysen and the baby. Hurry back," I said looking at the blunt.

"I don't want to leave you in this state, Beast," Sin said placing her hand on my shoulder. "Talk to me."

"I'll be okay, gone now and get back here in one piece. Don't be driving reckless and don't forget to get the car seat and the bag that we packed for the both of them," I said fighting to keep my voice strong.

"I have everything already by the door. I'll be back within the hour and I want to know what the fuck is going on as soon as I get back," she said kissing me fully on the lips and left out leaving me alone once again. When I heard the front door close, I let out the breath I was holding and threw the tumbler that sat on my desk against the wall.

"Muthafucka!" I screamed out loud. "How the fuck didn't I see this shit going on? There's no way he should've had to go through that type of shit!"

The tears streamed down my face but the hate in my heart grew by the second and I was ready to wrap my hands around that nigga's throat. Big Jim was in the best place that one in his shoes could be, he was the luckiest muthafucka living. I kept reaching to press play and I couldn't will myself to do so.

Drinking straight from the bottle, I got up and went back to Sin's stash and just brought the whole muthafuckin' unicorn downstairs. That's where she kept what she called her medicine, in a glass fuckin' unicorn. I would just have to replace her shit because I was about to smoke my ass off.

***

I don't know how long I sat staring at nothing. The sound of the doorbell brought me back to reality and I struggled to stand to my feet. My body felt like I was floating instead of walking. That's how high I was. As I looked out the peephole, I could see my nephews on the other side and unlocked the door.

"Damn Beast, what the fuck is going on? You looked like you been smoking since this morning," Rodrigo joked as I stepped to the side so they could enter. "Shit, you smell as if you drank all the liquor in your stash."

"A bit of both actually. Y'all gon' want to smoke and drink too when y'all hear what the fuck I've heard. I still can't believe the shit but it came from the source's mouths and I won't repeat none of it. Just know, things will not be the same after this. I won't be able to tell y'all what to do or when to do it. I'm backing y'all one hundred percent from this point on."

"Yo', you talking in riddles, nigga. None of that shit made any type of sense," Ricio said turning to me.

"Follow me to my office, I'll let you hear for yourself," I said leading the way. I sat down in my chair and connected the projector so we all could watch the footage without crowding around my desk. They pulled up chairs and faced the back wall waiting for whatever I had to reveal. "What y'all about to see is disturbing. All I can say is, don't tear up my shit. I'm the only one that can do that," I said starting the footage.

When we got to the point where I'd stopped, both Rodrigo and Ricio jumped to their feet! I knew if I reacted the way I did, they were going to be ten times worse. "Stop that shit, nigga!" Ricio shouted. "Did this muthafucka just say that he wanted my brother to suck his dick?" he asked fuming.

"Yeah, you heard that shit right, Ricio. I'm pissed because we had to learn about this shit now. Did either one of you have any suspicions of this going on?" I asked.

"Nigga you must be outta yo' muthafuckin' mind! Big Jim would be dead as fuck had I known he was doing that sick ass shit to my baby brother. Don't ask me no shit like that ever again! The real question is why the fuck *he* didn't tell us?"

"That's something we will never know the answer to, Rodrigo. Let's listen to what else this bitch has to say," I said reaching for the play button.

"I'm not about to sit here and listen to this shit! My brother was not a fuckin' homo, brah!" Ricio yelled kicking over the chair.

"We know that, Ricio," Angel chimed in. "I think we should keep watching to see if he gives any clues in his words, cuz. As painful as it may be, we have information that can be used. Knowing his hoe ass violated the lil homie has already cost him his life. This muthafucka being in jail means nothing, he can still get touched. Sit down and bear through whatever else we're about to hear."

Ricio stood with his arms folded and waited for me to start the footage back up. I knew how he was feeling and didn't want to continue watching either, but I knew we had to. The discussion afterwards was what I was looking forward to because they took this shit to a whole other level.

"I did that shit because your daddy was a bitch ass nigga! You were paying for him treating me like a low budget street nigga. I got at his ass when I had his muthafuckin' head blown off and took over his shit. I chose you to take this dick up the ass because I'm still pissed at him. Since I couldn't bring his ass back to life and kill him again, I opted to fuck his weak ass son and get away with it.

You will continue to do what the fuck I say and you better not tell a soul what the fuck I had you doing. Am I clear?"

"Nah, you not clear. You won't stop what the fuck is planned for my brothers, that means I have to ruin yo' ass in return. Everything you did to me will be known in the streets. I don't give a damn

*what people think happened, or if they think I'm gay. The truth will
be told.*

*Don't think I don't know that yo' ass is a down low nigga be-
cause I do. There were plenty of nights I heard you and that nigga
Floyd moaning passionately in each other's ears. You had a whole
nigga but you wanted to fuck with me!"*

*"Somebody is mad now, huh? I'm gon' tell you this, Maxie. If
you think you are going to put my business in the street without any
repercussions, think again. You are one dead man walking right
along with yo' brothers. Don't go back to my house, you no longer
live there.*

*I hope you saved up some money because yo' dealing days are
over with me. You can starve to death and I wouldn't give a fuck.
The first person that says Big Jim is a homo, your head is going to
be delivered to your muthafuckin' brothers in a cardboard box.
Don't ever bring yo' ass back around me, nigga! Chuck let me out
of here before I kill this punk!*

Big Jim was led out of the room and Max sat up straight in the
seat with his chest poked out. Ten minutes later he was walking out
of the room and the screen went blank. I stopped the disc and closed
my laptop and folded my hands on top of it.

"I'm killing that nigga whenever I get the chance! This shit is
sick as fuck and I bet my life Floyd touched him too!" Ricio yelled.
"There's no way his ass didn't know what the fuck was going down.
But I guarantee his ass gon' pay for his wrong doing and his fuck
buddy's."

"Where are these muthafuckas hidin' out at?" Rodrigo's voice
boomed throughout the room. "I need to know now!"

"Rodrigo, we gotta get a plan in order—"

"Beast, fuck yo' plan! I've been sitting in wait too muthafuckin'
long. Hearing the shit that happened to my brother hurt a nigga! I
didn't know shit about what the fuck was going on and Floyd and
his minions won't breath the same air as me another day! I don't
give a damn what time it is when I see them niggas, it's lights out!
Ya'll can sit and plan out all ya'll want, I'm going out full throttle.

If I have to comb the whole muthafuckin' Southside, I'm drawing blood tonight," he said storming from my office.

"Rodrigo, hold up!" Ricio said running behind him. He came back faster than he left with a grim look in his eyes. "He pulled off before I could get to him. We have to try to stop him, man."

"Ain't no stopping him. Rodrigo's been wanting to draw blood for the longest. The aftermath starts now," I said shaking my head.

"I gotta get back to the motel to figure out what to do with Slim. I think I'm just gon' have to put him in a treatment center. Shit is about to be hot and I need to be out in these streets with y'all. I don't have time to deal with him right now," Ricio said pacing back and forth. "They were fuckin' my damn brother man!"

"Who was fuckin' what brother, Ricio?" Sin asked from the doorway. She must've come in while Ricio was screaming and no one heard her.

Madysen appeared behind her holding the baby and I knew I didn't want to reveal shit in front of her. "Nobody Sin," I responded.

"Fuck that, Beast! Secrets has been kept long enough. She has a right to know!" Ricio spat at me. He turned back to Sin and a tear fell from his eye. "Big Jim was forcing Max to do shit he wasn't supposed to be doing—"

The impact frightened the baby and he started crying. "Madysen, take the baby and get him settled. "I said looking pass Sin. She had the look of disgust on her face and I knew then she wouldn't hold herself together. "Sin, take the baby from her."

Madysen didn't put up a fight when Sin removed the baby from her arms. "I knew something was going on with him. He would only touch me when he came in late at night and it seemed like he had a point to prove. He was forcing himself to be with me because he was gay," Madysen sobbed dropping to her knees.

"My brother wasn't gay! He was forced to do that shit and it had been going on for years according to him. Nobody knew what Big Jim's nasty ass was doing and Max was too scared to say anything about it. He was afraid muthafuckas like yo' ass would label him! Don't ever let me hear you say that shit again, Madysen!"

"Ricio, you are in denial! While I thought Max was out trickin' off with other women, he was out sucking dick!" she yelled at him.

Before I could stop Ricio he had stalked over to where Madysen sat and slapped the shit out of her. "Watch yo' mouth bitch, because you don't know what the fuck you're talking about! I'll kill yo' muthafuckin' ass and save you the trouble of doing it yourself."

"Ricio, that's a muthafuckin' female!" I snarled at him. Angel jumped up and grabbed him around his waist restraining him from striking her again.

"It's okay, Beast, he didn't hurt me. Nothing could hurt me more than knowing the man that I gave my all too was on the down low and loved dick just as much as I do. I cried so many nights because he didn't answer his phone or when he came to my house smelling like sex. Not to mention fucking me like a whore instead of his girlfriend. I let it go because I loved him.

Do you know how that makes me feel knowing he's been with men? Let me tell you, it feels nasty as fuck! You can stand there praying it all away, but face the fact, Ricio, the truth can't be erased," she said rising to her feet before she walked to her bedroom and slammed the door.

"Ricio, I'm sorry. They will pay for this shit," Sin said as Ricio hurried through the house and out the door with Angel on his heels.

"I should've kept this shit to myself, Sin. Both of them are about to tear this city apart," I said looking down at the baby she held in her arms. "And I will be going to war right beside them." Kissing her on the temple, I went upstairs to process everything.

Meesha

Chapter 16
Rodrigo

I was speeding on the expressway like I was racing in a Daytona 500 race. Finding Floyd was the only thing on my mind and sleep wouldn't come until I drew blood. Slowing down as I spotted a state trooper, going to jail for speeding was not something I was about to eat. I'd rather go for blowing a nigga's brain's out the back of his head.

As I got closer to the city, my trigger finger started tingling and I knew, somebody's mama was going to be getting black dress ready. Ricio didn't give me much to go on about where Floyd set up shop, but I knew who did know. I reached into my pocket while keeping my eyes on the road and pulled out my phone. I found AK's contact info and hit him up. He seemed to answer as soon as the phone started ringing.

"Man, Rodrigo, where the fuck is Ricio? This nigga throwing up green shit and I think he's dying," he said panicking.

"AK, that nigga is throwing up that shit, he'll be good. You got to let that shit take its course. I'm on my way to you and I will stop and get some bananas, Gatorade, and something for that nigga to eat. I left Ricio at Beast's house. We just found out some shit that fucked me all the way up. I need the info on Floyd and them Southside nigga's but it can wait until I get there."

"Hurry up man, I think this nigga needs to be in the hospital. This can't be normal, for real."

"Aight, I'm on my way. I won't even stop at the store. I'm coming straight to you. Hold tight, fam," I said ending the call.

I made it to the motel in about fifteen minutes. An ambulance was parked in front of the hotel room and AK was standing outside. Pulling into a parking spot, I hopped out and ran over to him.

"What the fuck happened in the short amount of time it took me to get here?"

"I told you he was throwing up green shit when I talked to you. He fell to the floor holding his stomach. He was screaming loud as fuck and he started shaking uncontrollably and his eyes rolled to the back of his head. When he stopped shaking, he started rocking while still holding his stomach and told me to call an ambulance.

His words were, 'the only way I can beat this shit is if I go to a center. If I stay here, I'll die. Reese wanted this for me and I have to do it for him.' So, I did what he asked and now he's in the back of the ambulance and they are about to take him away," AK said running down everything to me.

I went to the ambulance and asked the paramedic if I could talk to Slim for a moment. She was taking his blood pressure and he seemed kind of out of it. "You have to be quick about it, we have to get him to the hospital, sir."

"Okay, thanks," I said climbing inside. "Slim, you gon' be good fam. We got you, here's my number, hit me when you are settled at the hospital so we'll know what's going on with you. Put me down as your next of kin too," I told him as I put my card in his pocket.

"Find them, Youngin'. They need to be dealt with now! I'm gonna get through this, just hold everything down until I get back," he said before he started breathing funny.

"You have to let us get to the hospital, sir. He needs medical attention now!" the paramedic said as she checked his heartbeat.

"Stay with us, Slim!" I yelled as the doors closed in my face. The ambulance raced out of the lot with the sirens blaring. Mercy Hospital was the closest to the motel and I knew that's where they were headed. I couldn't worry about that at the moment because I had other fish to fry. I'd wait until Slim or the hospital staff hit me with an update.

"Aye, trail me to Psycho's crib. The three of us about to slide on these niggas. You know where they're setup at, right?" I asked AK when I got back to where he was standing.

"Yeah, Floyd led me right to all his spots. I'm down for whateva. Precious stay ready, nigga."

"That's what I'm talking about. Let's go."

I jumped in my ride as I waited for AK to lock up the room. Finding Psycho's number on my phone, I hit the button to call him up. He answered sounding as if he had a lot on his mind.

"What up, Fam?"

144

"You at the crib? I need you to take a ride with me."

"Yeah, what's going on?" he asked.

"I'll explain when I get there."

"Say less, my nigga."

Throwing my phone into the cup holder, I pulled out of the spot and headed to my destination. AK was behind me and I hit the button and a song started playing on the radio that had me shakin' my head.

Stop cappin', I'm really popping
How can I slip if I'm the one doing the mopping?
No forensics, no witness, no ballistics
No attachment, but this Glock got extensions

Glancing down at the display to see who the hell was rappin' about the life he read about, just like I figured, a nobody. Some young nigga named Blueface that I'd never heard of and I knew why too. All of these raps nowadays sounded the same talking about the same shit, where's the originality. I was a young nigga but I'll stick to my old school rap before I listened to that bullshit. Finding an Old School Rap station, Nas' track *NY State of Mind* blared through my speakers and I bumped that shit as I cruised down Martin Luther King Drive.

It took fifteen minutes for me to pull up to Psych's crib on 69th and King and I found a spot right out front. AK had to park a few cars ahead of me and stood waiting for me to get out. My phone vibrated and I pulled it from my hip. It was Ricio but I wasn't trying to allow him to clock my moves so I let the call go to voicemail.

Psycho came out locking up his crib and descended the steps. "Talk to me. Where we headed?" he asked with a frown.

"The shit I learned got a nigga's mind blown. I'm telling y'all because y'all family and this is where the shit shall remain," I said glaring at both of them.

"Nigga, we know the code. The enemy ain't in our circle, you ain't gotta worry about shit getting out. If it's that deep, we getting' at the niggas behind the bullshit," AK growled. "Spit that shit and stop studying the muthafuckas that ain't did shit but proved loyalty."

"Big Jim violated Max in the worse way. Beast's inside connect at the prison gave sound evidence of Max's last visit with that nigga and it revealed that he was raping my lil brother." I was embarrassed as fuck telling them that shit, but I was ready to knock the fuck outta whoever started judging.

"You lying, right?" AK said with his nose flaring wildly.

"Nah, I wish I was. That's one of the reason's we're going to eliminate whoever the fuck we see when we roll up outside their new traps. Hearing that booty bandit laugh about what he did to my brother, gave the word murder a new meaning. He gave no fucks about his actions and seemed proud of himself. I'm gon' keep his same energy when I don't give a fuck about mine."

"Oh, hell nawl! I don't want to hear shit else! Let's go!" AK yelled heading for his truck. "We riding together. He said pulling the driver's door open to his truck and hopped in.

AK was pissed but not as much as myself. My anger wasn't showing but my trigger finger was itching like a muthafucka. I was waiting to lash out at the right time and that would be when I laid eyes on anybody from Floyd's crew. All I had to do was wait for AK to point out the one's he saw that nigga talking to when he followed him.

Once we were all inside the truck, AK pulled off with Precious propped against his leg. I glanced in the side mirror on the passenger side and noticed a car behind us. AK made a right on 71st and King Drive and the car did the same. That's when I noticed it was a DT car.

"Aye, fam. Twelve's behind us, we all dirty in this muthafucka. Is the compartment in the floor unlocked, AK?" I asked keeping my eye on the two white muthafuckas in the Crown Vic.

"Yeah. Push the lever and it should open right up," he explained as he kept driving the speed limit.

"Hand me the choppa, AK. Rodrigo give me your shit and I'm duckin' mine too," Psych said moving smoothly so it wouldn't look like we were on bullshyt.

"Lock that bitch and make sure the mats are in place. They are really on my ass," AK said hitting his turn signal to make a left onto

Indiana. "Yeah, they're waiting for an opportunity to pull my black ass ova."

As soon as he made the turn, the law hit their lights and AK pulled over. I sat in the seat calmly and watched these two bastards exit their car with hands on their guns. "Look at this shit," I said under my breath. "They ready to shoot a nigga, white muthafuckas."

One of them went to AK's side of the car and the other came around to my side. I wasn't worried about nothing because they weren't going to find shit. The officer on my side pointed a flashlight inside the car in Psycho's face and then around the back of the car.

"Pierre Banks?" the officer asked Psycho through the window.

"That's me. What the fuck you looking for me for?"

"Can you step out of the car? I have a couple questions I want to ask about your father Rodney Banks."

"Nah, I can't get out the car, you can talk to me from here," Psycho replied without moving.

"I asked you nicely, now I'm telling you. Get the fuck out of the car, boy!"

"Get out the car, fam. I got ya back, ain't shit gon' happen to you," I said calmly. "Hear what they gotta say so we can move the fuck around." Psycho opened the door and stepped out of the car. The other officer peered over and shined his light in my face.

"If it ain't the infamous Mr. Vasquez," he laughed. "I've been looking for you since you made your debut on the Channel Nine news. I need to holler at you, bro."

"Nigga, you white, I'm black. We ain't the same," I laughed at his goofy ass. "I will never be yo' muthafuckin' bro, *brah*."

"I'm Detective Bradley—"

"*So*. What the fuck you been looking for me for? I ain't got shit foe yo' ass."

"I believe you do. Step out the car for me," he said walking in front of the car and around to the passenger side door. He snatched it open and I had my phone in my hand recording his ass. "Put the phone away, please."

147

"Nah, if you want to talk to me, all this shit will be on record. It's not against the law to record you muthafuckas. Not that the shit holds up in our defense anyway but I'm not putting it down. As you can see, it's not a weapon so don't try to use that 'he got a gun shit," I smirked.

"We're not here to hurt anyone. We just want answers to some of the questions we have. Sir, you can get out the car as well," Detective Bradley said to AK. "We may as well question all of you at once. Keep your hands where I can see them as you get out. Don't do anything stupid and everything will be okay and we all will go about our merry way."

AK's temple was throbbing and I could tell he was about to blow up so I put my leg out the door and nodded my head at him. He followed suit and got out the truck leaving the door opened. AK walked around to where I was standing and crossed his arms over his chest.

"Pierre, are you aware that your father was found burned to death in his home last week?" Detective Bradley asked.

"Nah, I haven't talked to my father. He's a busy lawyer so when he has time, he contacts me," Psych replied nonchalantly. "We haven't been close in a while so it's not uncommon if I don't hear from him."

"You don't sound heartbroken hearing that he passed away. Maybe you know what really happened to him," The other Detective sneered.

"Cooper!" Detective Bradley shouted his partners name. "This is not how you get information dammit!"

"I'm tired of playing good cop to these thugs, Bradley! They are going to talk regardless. The choice is not theirs, it's ours!"

I wanted to reach out and snatch that nigga's Adam's apple from his throat. He was tough with these weak niggas but he had never had an encounter with me. He had the game fucked up. "See, Officer Pig, that's where you muthafuckin' wrong. I'm not your average nigga. I don't bow down to no muthafuckin' body and death is not something I'm afraid of facing.

148

Your hand hasn't come off the butt of your gun since you got yo' punk ass out of that car. I want you to know if you plan to use it, you better make that shot count. Now, fam said he didn't know shit about his father passing away until yo' prick ass mentioned it! Where the fuck is the compassion?" I pointing the camera in his direction.

"I wasn't addressing you, Smart Ass! Get against the fucking car now!"

"Cooper, protocol dammit! You're going about this all wrong!" Detective Bradley screamed at his partner. "Let me handle this. Go sit in the car!"

Cooper snatched his phone from his hip as he glared at me. Walking back to the Crown Vic, I could see his lips moving a mile a minute as he glanced back over his shoulder. AK and Psych were leaning against the truck without worry as I stood straight up like the G I was destined to be.

"Mr. Banks, I offer my sincere condolences." I laughed out loud when Bradley said that shit because there was no type of sincerity in his words. We knew he only wanted answers so he tried to say whatever he could to get them. "You didn't know about the passing of your father but what do you know about your brother getting shot last Friday?"

"My brother? I'm an only child! What the fuck are you on, brah. I can't tell you shit about whoever you inquiring about."

Psycho lied his ass off with a straight face. Detective Bradley stared at him trying to read him for any signs of fabrication. "You don't know Rodney Banks Jr.? he asked skeptically.

"I know of him now that you mentioned the name. All my life I've only known one Rodney and that's my father. I don't have any other siblings that I know of," Psych told him.

"Word on the street is you used to run with Floyd and his crew. Rodney "Shake" Banks Jr. is affiliated with those same people. How is it you didn't know he was related to you?"

"Nigga, I just told you I didn't know about that shit! I didn't know that nigga was my fuckin' brother and I don't run with no muthafuckin' crew! My peeps are family!"

"Okay, calm down. I'm just trying to get to the bottom of this puzzle that's not coming together."

"It's not my job to help you do your job. I don't have shit for you on any of the shit you questioning me about. If you don't have nothing else to talk about, we out of here because y'all pulled us over for bullshit anyway. Stop listening to what you heard in the streets and go out there to get the real fuckin' criminals and leave us the fuck alone."

As Psycho finished reading the Detective, the sound of sirens could be heard loud and clear. Before I could turn my head there were about six squad cars coming down Indiana in both directions. Cooper got his pink ass out of the car with a smirk on his face and I knew then he was on one. The boys in blue jumped out with their guns drawn, typical police shit of course. All three of us were thrown against the truck and we complied without resisting.

"Nah, leave the two of them alone, they're okay. It's that big mouth asshole that I want down at the station," Cooper said walking up with his finger extended in my direction.

"Fuck you, nigga! You had to call for backup with all that shit you was talking," I laughed at his ass. "You a pussy!" I said as my arms were snatched behind my back and the cuffs locked around my wrists.

"Watch how you to talk to an officer of the law," the cop said slamming my head into the truck.

"You a bitch too! Why wait to manhandle me while my hands are behind my back. Take these cuffs off so you can try that shit again," I sneered. "Stupid muthafucka's ain't shit without those guns and a badge!" I was escorted to the nearest squad car and the lump was growing on my forehead but my blood was boiling and my inner nigga was ready to fuck some shit up.

Call my people and tell 'em what's up, they may try to kill a nigga. If I'm not out in a couple hours find my ass!" I was able to shout out before my head was pushed down and I was forced into the back of the car.

Chapter 17
Latorra

Nervousness had set in the pit of my stomach as I walked through the doors of the DNA Diagnostic Center on Ridge Avenue. The facility wasn't hard to find but I didn't like the hour-long commute from one end of the city to the other. The entire ride I had to talk myself out of turning around and saying fuck taking the test but, it had to be done and I was already there. People of all nationalities were sitting in wait and many didn't seem too thrilled to be there. A Caucasian woman was sitting with tears rolling down her face as the man beside her let the entire room know she was a hoe.

She was holding an infant child that couldn't be no older than a month in her arms, rocking back and forth. I made my way to an empty seat along the wall when his voice boomed loudly for everyone to hear. Shit, I got scared for a minute myself as I sat down.

"We wouldn't be in here if you hadn't opened your legs trying to pin a baby on me. I'm white as fuck. How do you expect me to be happy to say this dark ass baby is mine, Sara? There's no way this is me and you know this. You didn't think I knew about your trips to the westside, did you?

This proves everything that was brought to my attention. You crying because your cover is blown. The truth shall set you free. We don't have to take this test to reveal what I already know."

"This is your baby! I want to prove that to you, that's why we're here!" the Sara girl cried.

"Get yo' money back, shawty. I've been sitting listening to homeboy and he is standing tall on his shit. Then, I look at you, him, and the baby, I'm sorry to inform you, ain't no way that's his baby," a guy said shaking his head. "That baby got a whole lot of melanin in its skin, white folks don't have none of that. Shid, yo' baby could be my lil cousin," he laughed.

"Shut the fuck up! You don't know what the fuck you're talking about. This is his baby and he know it. We all have a touch of black in us, we are going to take this test and prove what I already know," Sara screamed.

"Don't get mad at me. You should be mad at ya'self for thinking you could pull the wool over dude's eyes and pass that baby off as his own. Ray Charles can see that baby belongs to a nigga! Yep, I said it. That's Bobby Johnson baby like a muthafucka. Justin Timberlake had nothing to do with that so stop lying. If it was me, I would've bust yo' muthafuckin' head to the white meat."

"Latorra Smith!"

I couldn't get out the chair fast enough to get away from the circus act that was taking place in front of me. The security guard wasn't shit because he stood in the corner laughing. How about stop it because it was distasteful in the workplace.

"Follow me," the technician said leading me through a door and down the hall. "Take a seat in here and I will be back in a few minutes."

"How long is this process?" I asked trying to get an idea of how long I would be there.

Looking down at the folder in her hand, she flipped through a couple pages before she raised her head. "The test itself will not take too long, maybe ten minutes tops."

"When should I expect the results?"

"Well it looks like a James Carter paid for express processing. The results will be sent to the email you provided on the original form."

"I didn't fill out any form. I was called with a date, time, and location. Is there any way I can fill that form out as well? I really need to know the results at the same time as Mr. Carter," I asked nicely. Fuck he thought? I needed to see what the results were, not something he wanted me to know.

"Sure, I'll bring it back when I return. Sit tight," the technician said as she left the room.

I was trying to figure out why I wasn't given the information to receive the results. Something wasn't right about this whole DNA thing. Out of nowhere, a nigga in jail tells me that he thinks he's my father. James Carter is on some bullshit and I knew he was going to let it be known what his intentions were.

My phone rang loudly in my purse and I quickly retrieved it. Glancing down at the screen, I saw Mauricio's name on the display. I hadn't talked to him since he left my house after fucking me like I was a hoe. I was good on his ass so I let the call go to voicemail. He didn't let up and called again within seconds.

"What do you want?" I asked when I answered.

"Damn, is that how you answer the phone when somebody calls yo' ass? What the hell is wrong with you?"

"Don't act like everything is on the up and up with us. The way you left my house the other day was unacceptable."

"The way I left yo' house? Latorra I told you I had some shit to do—"

"Nah you fucked and left! I haven't heard from you or anything, Mauricio! I'm not that type of bitch that you have your way with, then call when it's convenient for you! Don't call me no mutha-fuckin' more, I'm done with you!" I said ending the call.

Mauricio called once more and I didn't bother to answer. A few seconds later I received a text from him but the technician entered the room and I dropped the phone in my purse without seeing what he had to say.

"Okay, we can start this process now. My name is Sherri and I will be conducting the test for you today, sorry for the delay. Her is the form you requested. You can fill it out while I explain a few things to you. I have your test here and it's labeled with your name and its color coded so there won't be any mix-ups. First, I need to see your identification to make sure you are who you say you are."

Handing her my state ID, I started filling out the form while she compared the name to the one on the envelope. After I finished with the form, I handed it back and she passed me my ID. Sherri walked to the sink and began washing her hands. She grabbed a couple paper towels before snatching a pair of latex gloves from the box. As she sat down before me, she slipped the gloves over her hands.

"Alright, these are the swabs that I'll be using to collect the sample that's needed," she said showing me the packaging. "The way to open the package is from the bottom because you don't want to touch the cotton swab and contaminate it. Your name is on this as well so we would know it belongs to you. I'll start by swabbing your inner cheek to collect the skin cells. Open up for me so I can get you out of here."

I opened my mouth and Sherri began rotating the swab along my cheek. Using circular motions, she twirled the swab about twenty times before slipping the swab in another envelope and sealing it tightly. Picking up a pen she stood in front of me and handed the envelope to me.

"I want you to initial here," she said pointing to the line at the bottom of the envelope. "This lets us know that you gave consent for us to test your DNA. It is also the last step in the process. Like I explained earlier, you will get an email of the results within an hour or two. Do you have any questions for me?" She asked as I wrote my initials.

"No, you have answered all the questions I had already."

"Well you are good to go. Enjoy the rest of your day, Miss Smith."

"Thank you, and same to you," I said standing from the chair.

Hoisting my purse on my shoulder, I followed the signs back to the front of the facility. My mind was filled with worry, wondering what would happen if this man was really my father. I walked slowly to the parking lot where my car was park and once again my phone starting chiming from inside my purse. I ignored it until I was settled behind the wheel.

I fished around blindly until I located my phone but by that time, it stopped ringing. The caller was James Carter and I wasn't going to return his call because I wasn't ready to talk to him. To me, he was too eager to find out if he was my father. James wasn't taking into consideration that him having a phone in prison and my affiliation with him could put me in a bad situation. As far as I'm concerned, I didn't know anything about his ass and I would deny the shit in a heartbeat.

Inserting the key into the ignition, I started my car and put the gear in reverse. Once again, my phone rang in my hand, making me put pressure on the brake pad. James was calling and I knew if I didn't answer, he would continue trying to reach me.

"Hello," I answered drily.

"Damn, Latorra, why haven't you returned my calls? I've been trying to get in touch with you since last week. Did you go take the test?" he asked agitatedly.

"I'm not obligated to answer nor return your calls. There's nothing to discuss between us until the results come back. I feel you have shady intentions with all of this anyway."

"How do you figure that? Look, I'm only trying to get to know you since deep down I know you're my daughter. I can't imagine what you had to go through after your mother passed away. I can't go back in time to change what happened in your life, but we can try to build from here on out."

I wasn't trying to hear any of the shit he was spitting. All I wanted to know was his motive for getting this test so quickly. He didn't do much of anything to find me back in the day. But here he was, ready to step up to be daddy when I was grown as fuck.

"Why didn't I get the proper paperwork from the DNA center? You thought I was supposed to take your word on what the results were?" I asked angrily.

"I wasn't trying to get over on you. First of all, I didn't have an email for you. Secondly, I didn't want your name associated with me behind these prison walls. You work in the prison with the person that had to be in the room when I gave the sample and they also had to look at the paperwork. I gave them your name as the other recipient, via email.

Now, if you filled out the paperwork, that's fine by me. I did what was necessary to protect you and your job from the muthafuckas in here. If you would've answered yo' phone this wouldn't even be up for discussion."

I didn't even have a comeback for what he said because he was right. I felt a little better once he explained things but I still had my guard up. "When are you coming back to work? I've noticed you haven't been here since the day we talked," he said breaking the silence.

This muthafucka was checking my moves and I didn't like it one bit. "You wouldn't see me because I don't usually work that

Block. Even if I was at work, you wouldn't know about it," I threw back at him.

"That's where you're wrong. I know for a fact you haven't been to work. Don't let this test get in the way of your money. No nigga wants a female that don't have a job. It will bring problems into the relationship so you should always pave the way for yourself."

"I'm not in a relationship. That doesn't pertain to me. I had personal time to take off and that's exactly what I did, took the time to get my mind right. I'll get paid for the days I missed, why are you worried about my funds anyway? Look, hit me when the results are in. I'm trying to get home and relax. Plus, I have a long drive ahead of me."

"Latorra, I want you to know that I'm trying to make up for lost time—"

"You can't make up for shit because we don't even know what the results are! Save it until we see the writing in black and white. Until then, I'm done with this conversation. Bye, Mr. Carter," I said hanging up on his ass. I took the time to check my messages and opened the one Mauricio sent to me.

Mauricio: Look Shawty. I'm sorry if you feel I did you dirty but that wasn't the case. I had to move around because I had some shit to handle. To be honest, I didn't even come over to have sex with you. If I'm not mistaken, you initiated that shit and I finished it. Get out your feelings because you got what you wanted and I got a nut in return. Hit me up when you got your mind right.

His ass had his nerve turning the situation on me like he didn't want it. Throwing my phone in my purse, I eased my foot off the brake as I slowly backed out of the parking spot. Heading toward the expressway, I got madder as I thought about the way Mauricio treated me.

It took an hour and a half for me to get back to the Southside due to traffic. There was construction going on downtown and I got stuck in the middle of the afternoon rush. When I finally made it to my home, I was tired as hell. Kicking my shoes off at the door, I went straight to my bedroom and undressed. The shower and a nap were calling my name and I couldn't wait to crawl under my sheets.

Quickly washing my body several times, I stepped out of the shower and wrapped a plush towel around myself. Sleepiness took over soon as I stepped into my bedroom. Drying the access water off, I grabbed my phone out of my purse and pulled the covers back on my bed. As I laid back on the pillow, a notification appeared on my phone. When I looked down the first words I saw were, DNA Diagnostic Center.

My hands started shaking and I became nervous rather quickly. I took several deep breaths to control my breathing before I opened the email but it didn't work. The air around me felt as if I was being smothered by an invisible spirit of some kind. Placing the phone on top of the blanket, I got out of bed and went to the kitchen to get a cold glass of ice water.

It was hard swallowing the liquid but I managed to get it down. After refilling the glass, I returned to my bedroom to face the truth of the test. Silently praying for negative results as I placed the glass on top of the coaster on the nightstand, I crawled back into my bed and picked up my phone. Opening the email, I read the first line and closed my eyes. I focused back on the document and began reading.

My name was at the top of the email along with my address and customer number. My name was listed as the child and James' name was listed as the alleged father. It listed our race and the specimen numbers and the dates the tests were taken. I noticed James took his test last Friday, while I had taken mine that very morning. My eyes roamed to the next line and I forced myself to continue reading.

The alleged father, James Carter, cannot be excluded as the biological father of Latorra Smith. Based on the genetic testing results, the probability of paternity is 99.99%.

I dropped the phone and tears ran down my face at rapid speed. I didn't want James Carter to be my father. Something deep inside my soul told me that my life was about to take a turn for the worse. Snuggling under the covers as I continued to cry. My phone started ringing but I didn't want to be bothered so I silenced it and powered it off before I let my sobs put me to sleep.

Meesha

Chapter 18
Madysen

Walking in hearing that Max was having sex with men made me sick to my stomach. Ricio slapping me truly didn't faze me. Learning Max was having sex with men hurt more than anything. We talked about everything but he couldn't tell me about what was happening to him. Knowing that Big Jim was having his way with the love of my life had me puking every time I thought about it.

I was glad Beast left and Sin was upstairs in her room with the baby. As much as I wanted to love on that handsome little boy, I couldn't. When I looked at him after I gave birth in the car, all I saw was the man that I would never lay eyes on again in life.

Giovanni Vasquez is what I named my baby but I didn't want anything to do with him. Especially after learning Max's secret. In the back of my mind, all I could think about was him growing up to be just like his father, gay. Ricio could holler he wasn't until the cows came home, but I knew.

Ignoring all the signs, I craved the love anyway he gave it to me. Now look at me. In love with a dead man and depressed as fuck. Yes, I didn't want to live but I was being forced to continue on in this cruel world. Being watched like a hawk every minute of the day was really getting on my nerves. I had to come up with a plan to get out of the watchful eyes of everyone around me.

After rinsing my mouth after another episode of vomiting, I dried my face with a paper towel and opened the door. As I walked into my bedroom, Sin was sitting in the rocking chair holding Giovanni in her arms. My attitude turned cold from the sight of him alone and I pivoted to leave, but Sin saw me before I could.

"Madysen, come bond with this baby. He needs to feel love from his mother," she said sincerely.

"Sin, I don't know if I can. I don't know how to be his mother. Hell, I don't know how to live life anymore."

"I'll teach you how to be his mother. It may seem like it's a hard task, but it really isn't. Come sit down and talk to me for a few minutes."

I walked over to the chair that sat next to the rocker and took a sit. The top of Giovanni's head was covered with lots of black silky hair. Sin had him dressed in a blue onesie with matching socks. Turning away from the sight before me, I focused on the changing table that was stocked with plenty of diapers, wipes, and other items for my baby. The whole clan made sure Giovanni had everything he needed upon his arrival and I was truly grateful.

"I'm sorry for how I've been coming down on you, Madysen. I shouldn't have said half of the things I said to you. The only reason I was so hard on you is because I give a fuck about your wellbeing."

"You sure have a hell of a way of showing you care. Nothing that came out of your mouth told me that you gave a fuck about me, Sin. What I gathered from you was the fact that you want to beat my ass. Why though? Why threaten to harm me because I saw the love of my life get gunned down right in front of me?

It was me that held Max's head while he gurgled with blood spewing from his mouth as he struggled to breathe. I was the one telling him to hold on, to fight because he would be alright. My face was the last thing he saw before he closed his eyes. All of this happened to me in a blink of an eye!

Did it ever occur to you that every time you said something harsh to me, it could've led me to close my eyes forever? When I said I didn't want to live, I meant that shit! I have nothing to live for!"

The tears welled in my eyes and I saw the sorrow in Sin's. It didn't do anything to change my mindset at all. I knew my days of living were ticking away by the minute but no one else knew. It didn't matter what was said, my mind was made up.

"Giovanni is who you have to live for, Madysen! I promise I will do anything in my power to make sure you're the best mother for this little boy. Max is already gone. One of you have to be here to love this baby and give him a life he would be proud of.

I'm sorry that Max was killed, I'm sorry that your world got turned upside, I'm sorry you had to find out what happened to Max the way you did. Shit I'm still pissed about it but we can't change any of that. I'm sorry for the things that I said to you. I'm here for you, Madysen and so is everyone else."

The baby stirred in Sin's arms and he started fussing. Looking down at him while Sin rocked him back and forth, I heard Max's voice whisper in my ear. "Love my son, Maddy. For the both of us." I closed my eyes as warm tears slid down my cheeks. In my head I responded, "I'll try," and reached out for Giovanni.

Sin had the biggest smile on her face as she handed him over to me. Giovanni opened his eyes, identical to his father's and they never left mine. That day I learned to change a diaper, feed my son, and watch him sleep. It was the first time I had smiled since Max died and it was all because of the little boy I gave birth to.

I didn't notice I'd fallen asleep until I woke up to the sound of baby Giovanni squealing. I sat up on the side of the bed and looked at the crib he was lying inside. Getting up, I walked the short distance to the crib and lifted him up. He looked at me and sneezed in my face. Cradling him in the crook of my arm, I took him over to the changing table and placed him on the pad.

Changing his diaper, I made sure to clean him the way Sin taught me and tossed the soiled diaper in the baby Genie bin. He started fussing again and I knew he was probably hungry. Carefully picking him up, I walked out of the room to the kitchen. When I opened the refrigerator there weren't any bottles premade for me to warm up.

That was something Sin didn't show me how to do and I panicked because Giovanni was crying harder. Going back into the bedroom to get his pacifier out of the crib, I tried rocking him. It wasn't working for me like it worked for Sin and I began to get frustrated. He didn't want the pacifier and kept spitting it out. I didn't know what to do.

"Please be quiet! I'm trying to help you but you have to give me a chance to figure it out!" I screamed out angrily. "Shut up!"

"Madysen, that's not going to stop him from crying," Sin said calmly walking into the room. "What are you having trouble with?"

"I think he's hungry. When I went to get a bottle for him, there wasn't any made in the fridge. I don't know how to mix the milk."

"Why didn't you come upstairs or text me to come down? You can't let his crying irritate you like that. Patience is the key to great parenting. It's going to take time for you to get used to caring for Giovanni. I'll be here every step of the way. Don't ever hesitate to ask for help."

"You're right. I didn't think about coming to you. I didn't mean to scream at him," I said wiping a tear from my face. "Can you please, teach me how to prepare his milk?"

"I can and I will. Place him in the bouncer seat and make sure the pillow supports his head. We will take him in the kitchen with us because you never want to leave him alone unless he's in the crib. Right now, we don't need him crying too much because his navel cord hasn't fallen off yet. Later today I will show you how to care for that too," Sin said as she watched me buckle the baby into the seat.

I followed her to the kitchen placing Giovanni on the table. "He is drinking about two ounces of milk right now so first you will get a four-ounce bottle. Fill it to this line with the baby water," Sin said pointing to the two-ounce mark on the bottle. "Next you will take a scoop of the powdered milk and dump it into the bottle and shake until the milk and water are mixed together. It's not hard at all.

You won't have to warm the bottle unless you make the milk and put it in the refrigerator. Other than that, the water is already lukewarm. Don't ever microwave the bottle to warm it up. It's not safe," She explained as she continued to shake the bottle. "Now feed my nephew so he can be happy again."

Doing as I was told, I lifted Giovanni from his bouncer and positioned him in the crook of my arm. He devoured the milk soon as I placed the nipple to his lips. His eyes started drifting closed after a few minutes and I removed the bottle from his mouth. Placing him on my shoulder, I patted him on his back and he belched before nestling his head closer to my ear.

"Thanks for showing me how to care for him, Sin. I appreciate it so much."

"No problem. If you need me, I'll be upstairs. I have to make a run in about an hour, will you be alright to care for Giovanni alone until I return?" she asked.

"Yeah, I should be alright. I think I can manage on my own for a bit," I said with a smile.

"I'm gonna trust you to do that. Don't make me regret leaving you alone, Madysen. The trust between us starts now. I want you to take control of your life again. I have faith in you."

"I'll be good, Sin. I promise."

She stared at me for a moment while rubbing the top of Giovanni's head before leaving us alone in the kitchen. I sat breathing in the scent of my baby with a lot on my mind. The promise I had made to Sin was solid for the time being, but I couldn't promise anything for the future.

Meesha

Chapter 19
Ricio

Angel and I were going to meet up with Sam to discuss being his connect. To get my mind off the shit that I found out about Max, I decided to push the meeting up. I called Beast to accompany us because I hadn't been able to reach Rodrigo since we learned what happened to Max. This deal was going to put us on the map to get this money and I was more than ready. We had plenty of product to sell and more where that came from once the clientele picked up.

Cruising through the downtown streets, I was letting Angel see what it was like in that part of the city. We would get a chance to see all of Chicago once we put all the bullshit behind us. Until then, he would see what he could at the moment.

"Ricio, can I ask you a question?" Angel said as I turned down Dearborn Street.

"Yeah, cuz speak ya shit."

"What do you know about this guy we're about to meet up with?"

"I know he's getting money on the Northside and got it on lock. His father used to fuck with my father heavy until he was killed about two years before my father was murdered. The most important thing I know is that he is about to buy his bricks from me and we gon' be good out here in a minute," I said looking over at him for a second.

"Cuz, I want you to do a thorough background check to see what these people are into before you get involved with them. You can't take their word on anything because they could be working for the police. You have to do your own investigation so you will know how to handle them accordingly."

"I hear what you're saying cuz, but I don't know shit about checking nobody's shit without getting the police on my team involved. There's some shit I just don't want them to know about the operation I'm about to build."

"I understand you on that and that's why you have me. Back home I was considered a computer geek, glasses and all until my

165

father discovered my talent and forced me into his illegal business. I learned a lot while I was in his care and I won't let you go down because somebody set you up. I'm gonna make sure you have a clean slate. Any situation can disappear and it won't get detected."

"Get the fuck out of here!" I laughed. Your Rico Suave looking ass ain't no damn computer geek."

"Not only am I a geek, I'm a man of many faces and I'll prove it to you with this cat. I need to go to the Apple Store and pick up a couple of computers then hit a few spots to get other equipment that I need. The last thing I will do is call my father to ship my shit back from home. I'd rather start over," Angel said with confidence.

"You serious, huh?" I asked as I pulled in front of the restaurant.

"As a heart attack. I got your back, Ricio and you are going to live a lavish life with me on your team. I promise," he said getting out of the car as the valet came to park my shit.

"Welcome to Trattoria No. 10, do you have a reservation?" The hostess asked as we entered.

"Yes, the reservation should be under Samuel Locket," I replied.

"Mr. Locket and another part of your party is already seated. Right this way, gentlemen."

We followed her to the back of the Italian restaurant that was quiet and elegant. The guests were well dressed and so were we. I had on a black Givenchy suit with a pair of black dress shoes to match.

Angel wasn't playing with them either in his cream Valentino suit with a maroon shirt that was unbutton and a pair of maroon red bottom shoes on his feet. His hair was cut low and he had on a pair of shades that covered his eyes. Cuz looked like one of those exquisite Fortune 500 dudes that had millions.

"Your daddy was a good dude and it seems you've picked up his knack for business," Beast was saying to Sam as we approached the table.

"Mauricio, my man! Long time no see," Sam said standing when he saw me.

"Yeah, it's been a while," I said giving him a brotherly hug. "This is Angel, one of my business partners. He will be the person you work closely with," I said introducing my cousin.

"What's up, man," he said shaking his hand.

"Have a seat. Me and Beast were just talking about our dad's and how he used to beat my ass," he laughed.

"That's all good. Y'all can finish talking, we have time," I said taking a seat on the right of Sam and Angel on the left.

"No, we're here to discuss business, lets get down to it," Sam said eagerly. "I'm looking to cop thirty bricks a month, for now. It won't be a problem getting it off, but I want to see how the clientele will take the product first,"

I reached in my pocket and brought out the sample I knew I would need to win him over. "Here you go. When you want to do that because I'm confident about my shit?" I said sliding the baggie to him.

Angel was watching Sam like a hawk and so was Beast. He may have known his father, but like Angel said, we didn't really know Sam. He tested the product by rubbing a small amount along his gum line and instantly smiled. He was all in and I knew it.

"That shit's potent and I'm sold. Fuck that, I want fifty a month because that right there," he said pointing to the baggie. "Is gonna sell like hotcakes. Let's talk pricing."

"Just like you, I'm a businessman. I'm gon' give you the bricks at twenty G's a piece and you bring more clientele my way and the price sticks. Never talk prices to these niggas you send my way because the price for you, is for you. It ain't for everybody, understood?"

"Mauricio, I'm down with that and I got people all over that has been going through a drought because our connect up and disappeared. If you can handle the clientele, then we can do business," Sam said happily.

"My end is solid, don't worry about that, fam. When are you trying to get this thang started?" I asked.

"Tonight," he said reaching in his pocket. "This is the address to my warehouse. I will personally be there to accept the load and I will introduce you to my main man when you get there," he said looking at Angel.

"Be there in three hours, I'll be there alongside Angel to make sure everything runs smoothly. If there is ever a problem of any kind, we conduct business as men, not bitches. Communication is the key with any relationship and that line should always be open. Don't fuck over me and I won't have to kill you. I'm just keeping shit real with you."

"I understand completely and I appreciate your willingness to work with me. There are no snakes in my circle, guaranteed," Sam said rising to his feet with his hand held out for me to shake.

"Everybody got a snake slithering somewhere, it's on you to detect them before it's too late. Keep that in mind, man." I stood from my seat and sealed the deal with a handshake. "See you tonight and have my Mil ready for pickup. Don't be late. Beast, it was good seeing you."

He nodded his head as he sipped from his glass of water. I knew he had a plan because he didn't follow me out of the restaurant. He was on a mission of his own and I didn't need to know the dynamics until he found what he was seeking.

When valet retrieved my vehicle, Angel had a look of concern on his face when we got in. Giving him time to collect his thoughts, I started my ride and sat quietly. "Ricio, why is Beast still in there? Do we have to worry about him?"

I knew then that my cousin was going to be a great asset to the team. "Nah, Beast is family and thorough. He's doing what he does best. Observe, seek, find, and demolish if need be. He's the silence to our storm and I trust him with my life. The time to see him react, is coming very soon.

He's in there making sure all is well with the nigga I just made a deal with. It's good to have eyes and ears everywhere. Sam don't know how deep me and Beast roll. He won't find out until he fucks up," I smirked as I pulled away.

***

Angel and I went back to my crib to change before heading to the warehouse. I received a called from Psycho informing me that Shake had died moments before when he went to the hospital to see how he was doing. Another nigga down and a few more to go. Big Jim's team was dwindling true enough, but that didn't call for celebration just yet.

I also learned why Rodrigo wasn't answering his phone and with Sin on that detail, I was free to conduct this business before the bloody massacre began. "Aye, Angel you ready, cuz?" I hollered down the hall of my home.

"Yep," he said walking out the guest bedroom in a black jogging suit. "What's the plan?"

"We're heading to the warehouse to load the bricks then I'll call Sam before we head to the Northside. Everything should be easy breezy, cuz," I said as he looked at me skeptically. "Trust me," I explained descending the stairs.

"It's not you that I don't trust. There's something about this cat, I get a bad vibe about him and it's fuckin' with me because I didn't get a chance to check into his background."

"We good, stop worrying. Let's go make this drop then afterward we wait for more business to come our way. Since we've gotten this shipment out of the way, I can take you to get the equipment you need first thing Monday morning," I said leading the way to the garage.

The commute to the warehouse didn't take very long at all. When we pulled up the street was quiet as I got out to unlock the door. Angel was right beside me with his Glock in his hand. My cousin had my back to the fullest and I loved it.

"Stand right here, I'm gon' back the moving truck into the warehouse so we can load up."

"Aight, I got you," he said glancing around.

Unlocking the door of the U-Haul, I pulled the handle and jumped in. I didn't waste a moment as I inserted the key into the ignition. The engine turned with ease and I backed it up from the side of the warehouse and backed the truck in front of the door.

Throwing the truck in park, I exited so I could unlock the door to the warehouse.

"Angel, get in the truck and I will guide you in once I let up the door." I said rushing inside.

Disarming the alarm, I pushed the button to raise the door. Once it was raised completely, I yelled for Angel to back it up. "Okay, cuz, let's go!"

Angel got the truck in with no problem and I hit the button again to lower it. I grabbed the handle of the flatbed dolly that was along the wall and dragged it to the back where we kept the bricks. Keys in hand, I unlocked and pushed the door open.

"Damn, cuz! You muthafuckas doing it like this!" Angel exclaimed as he admired the room filled from floor to damn near ceiling with pure white.

"It's a lil sum' sum'," I shot back laughing. "We'll talk later, but for now, we need to get fifty of these bitches to the Northside in the next hour and a half. That gives us thirty minutes to get this shit loaded on the truck," I said walking into the room. "Each bundle has ten bricks in each. We will line them on that shelf in the back of the truck then secure them with the harness so they won't shift around.

It's gon' take both us to carry each bundle but we have to do it quickly. I hope you're in shape cause I'm not," I laughed.

"I'm ready," Angel said coming in to get the first bundle.

It didn't take as long as I thought to load the truck but my ass was winded. I needed to get my ass back in the gym because I shouldn't have been breathing like a fat muthafucka after lifting the bundles. Once the bricks were secured, we both hopped out of the truck and I locked the room before I walked to the front of the truck.

"You drive this baby out, and I'll lock up so we can roll," I said walking over to the wall to hit the button. The door went up and Angel pulled out and I hit the button again before I set the alarm and walked out of the warehouse. "Aight, let's go. I'll be your GPS system as you drive. Let's go get this money, cuz," I said happily.

We drove for about forty-five minutes before I took my phone out and hit Sam up. "I'm five minutes away, fam. I hope you ready."

"I'm here waiting on you. Pull up and we can handle things from there," Sam replied.

"Bet, see you in a minute." Ending the call, I looked at Angel, "drive past that muthafucka so I can see what it's looking like."

"I was gon' do that anyway, cuz. I don't trust this nigga," Angel grilled.

When we rode past Sam's warehouse, him and a couple other niggas were waiting just like he said they would be. Angel bent the block and parked in the dock area. Climbing out of the truck, Same walked to the passenger side and waited for me to exit.

"I thought that was you passing by but I wasn't sure," he laughed. "What happened, you got the address wrong?"

"Nah, I had to scope yo' ass out to make sure you wasn't trying to ambush a nigga," I said truthfully. "I don't think you trying to burn business with me, though."

"Why would you say that? I'm about this money, no grimy shit this way," Sam said rubbing his hands together as I stepped out of the truck. The two other dudes walked over and posted up alongside Sam. "I want you to meet Tank and Kilo. These are my two most trusted niggas but Tank will be the person that handles any transactions between us."

Shaking hands with them, I turned to introduce Angel. "You've already met my man Angel. He will be the go to person on this side. The two of y'all need to get acquainted because this is a money move for us all. We loaded this shit up, y'all on ya own with getting it out."

"We have no problem with that," Tank replied.

"Before we go any further, I need to see that dough," I said seriously.

"No doubt. Kilo go get the bags and let the door up. "Ricio, I may need you to back the truck up a little bit. You're too far out in the open," Sam said.

Angel gave me a look and nodded his head before coming out of his waistband with his Glock 50. Sam raised an eyebrow and cocked his head to the side. "What the fuck is that all about?" he asked.

"We ain't never did business with you before. I'm ready just in case some shady shit is on ya mind, homie," Angel shot back.

"I feel where you coming from, Angel this ain't that though. Me and Ricio go way back."

"That may be true. Where I'm from, I was always taught to expect the unexpected no matter the situation. If everything is good, there should be no problems, right?"

"You got it, fam," Sam said as the door rose on the hinges.

I was all for Angel standing locked and loaded. He was ready for whatever and I loved that shit. I got in the truck and backed it up until Sam motioned for me to stop. Kilo came out of the warehouse with two duffel bags and walked them over to Angel as I walked up.

"Here's the money, now let us do our part and we will be out of y'alls. hair," kilo said dropping the bags.

"I'm not going to count this shit but if it's a dollar off, we gon' have a problem," I shot back.

"There's a million dollars in those bags, Ricio. I have never stiffed a muthafucka in my life. Plus, I would never shit on the one that's helping me as much as I am him. This shit is solid," Sam replied with confidence. "Open up so we can get this shit rolling"

I unlocked the truck and stepped back. Angel grabbed the bags and put them in the front seat of the truck and came back and stood with his arms folded over his chest. When the last bundle was removed, I locked up as Sam came back out of the warehouse.

"I'll hit you when I'm in need of more. I hollered at one of my niggas in Detroit and I'm going up so he can sample what I already know he's gon' want. We in this together, Ricio so we gon' have to learn to trust one another," Sam said.

"I'll start trusting you when I feel everything is copasetic between us. Until then, this is business. Don't rush something after one transaction, if it was meant to be, it will be. I'm out, until next time homie," I said dapping him up. Angel on the other hand delivered a head nod and walked off.

"I don't trust that nigga, cuz," Angel said as I pulled off heading to the expressway.

Chapter 20
Sin

It was hard for me to even consider going out and leaving Madysen in the house alone with the baby. I didn't have a choice because I had to make some moves before Beast returned. The shit I walked in on about Max had me jalapeño hot. It hurt me to know that he was violated the way he was and there was no way I was going to sit back and act like it didn't happen.

As I put the finishing touches on my makeup, I admired myself in the mirror and was satisfied with the end result. My phone rang and I dug it out of my clutch to see who was calling, it was Psycho. I slid the bar to answer before I missed it.

"Hey, big head. What's going on?"

"Sin, I want you to know the police took Rodrigo down to the station."

"What do you mean they took him to the station? What for?"

"We were pulled over on 71st & Indiana by two detectives. They were questioning me about my father's death and on Shake getting shot. I kept telling them I didn't know anything about either incident but they kept trying to make it seem like I knew more than I was saying. Rodrigo of course, was giving them the business and one of the detectives called for backup. Me and AK was let go and they cuffed Rodrigo and put him in the car.

I'm not sure where they took him. Since we were on 71st, they may have taken him to the station on Cottage Grove. I know you are the lawyer of the family so I called you before anyone," he explained.

"Thanks for letting me know. Call Beast and Ricio to let them know what's going on. Inform them that you've already talked to me. There's nothing much I can do right now, but I will get over there as soon as I can. Lay low out there, shit is about to get hot. I gotta go, but I'll keep in touch."

"Bet. Talk to you soon," Psycho said ending the call.

"Damn, Rodrigo. Please don't do or say anything to incriminate yourself before I get to you, baby," I murmured to myself as I descended the steps. Making my way to Madysen's room, I knocked softly on the door before pushing it open. She was sleeping soundly and so was Gio. It was good to see she had him in the crib and not in bed with her. Easing back out of the room, I went to the garage and got into my ride.

I knew I wanted to make some shit happen, but I didn't know where to begin. I took my phone out of my clutch and dialed Psycho up again. When he answered, I didn't waste any time getting to the point.

"Hey, Psycho. What hospital is Shake in?"

"Sin, what are you about to do?" he asked.

"Mind yo' business, nigga and tell me what I need to know," I snapped.

"Let me go with you. I don't want to give you this information and something happens to you. Beast would never let me live if that happens."

"Fuck Beast! What muthafuckin' hospital is he in, Psych! I've been handling shit on my own since before you were thought of."

"Okay, he's at Metrosouth hospital on 129th. Be careful Sin."

I heard what he said but hung up without responding. I typed the name of the hospital into my google search to get the address. Once I obtained what I was looking for, I backed out of the garage and made my way to the expressway. It took about twenty minutes to get from my house to the hospital. As I got out of the car, I was thinking of a lie to get into Shake's room.

Walking toward the entrance, I saw Psycho standing in front of the hospital. I stalked over to him then slowed my pace. I couldn't be upset at him for coming to look out for me. When I stood in front of him, he started talking a mile a minute.

"Sin, I couldn't let you be out here by yourself. I had to come to make sure you were good. You needed me to get inside anyway, I'm his brother from what I was told anyway. They can't deny me entry because I'm part of his immediate family.

"It's alright. Let's just get in there to see what's going on with this nigga," I said walking pass him opening the door.

We walked to the counter together and the woman behind it greeted us sweetly. "Welcome to Metrosouth, how may I help you?" she asked.

"I'm here to see about my brother, Rodney Banks," Psycho responded.

The woman typed on the keyboard and looked up after finding the information she was looking for. "There are strict restrictions for Mr. Banks visitors. I will need a picture ID from the two of you and both of you must be family," she explained.

"I have my identification," Psycho said pulling his wallet out of his back pocket.

"What about you ma'am, do you have identification?" Placing my clutch on the counter, I sifted through my many cards and found my fake ID that I used when I was up to no good. Handing the card to her, we waited until she did her job and gave us visitor's passes. "Thank you, Mr. Banks and Mrs. Nesbitt. Rodney is in room 908. Take the elevators down the hall to your left."

"Thank you," Psycho said. "I hope this nigga is barely breathing when we get up here."

"They have him under radar so my plans of killing him today just went out the window. We're going to have to find a way to touch him without it leading back to us. For now, we will only go see him and play it by ear."

"Sin, your last name ain't Nesbitt—"

"Mind ya business, Psych. Mind ya business," I said stepping onto the elevator that awaited us as we walked up.

When we arrived on the ninth floor it was chaotic as hell. There were doctors and nurses scrambling around like ants. I was confused as to what the hell was going on. We couldn't move toward Shake's room because it was amongst all the ruckus.

"Room 908, get there now!" A doctor yelled.

"What's going on?" Psycho asked one of the nurses as she rushed pass us. "That's my brother's room."

"There's a code blue, that's all I can tell you at the moment, sir. I have to get in there to help your brother," she shot back over her shoulder.

"Damn, that muthafucka better not die before I get the chance to kill him," I mumbled under my breath. "Let's find a place to sit while they're working on him."

At that moment, Floyd was coming down the hall with his hands cradling his head. He looked spaced out and kept turning around glancing over his shoulder. Then walking back in the direction of the room. He paced back and forth as we watched him panic. Shake's condition couldn't have been good because that nigga had fear written all over his face.

Twenty minutes later the nurses and doctors slowly left the room. One of the doctors stopped and pulled Floyd to the side and was talking to him. He turned abruptly to the wall and punched his fist through the wall. Floyd's actions told me all I needed to know. Rodney "Shake" Banks Jr. was dead.

"Shake just died, Psych. We gotta get out of here before Floyd spots us," I said getting up to head to the elevators. "Call Ricio and Beast to let them know what just happened. I'm about to head over to the police station and pick up Rodrigo."

"Sin, I have a funny feeling something is about to go wrong. Another one of their men has died by our hands and they won't be sitting back much longer. At some point, they will be seeking revenge," Psycho said lowly as we stepped onto the elevator. "We also need to find out about those Southside niggas. We knew about the crew on the westside, but we've offed the majority of them already."

"We will be having a meeting very soon. With Shake dying, we need a plan A, B, and C as soon as possible. You didn't mention me coming here to Beast, did you?" I asked as we walked through the lobby after exiting the elevator.

"I wanted to but I decided to come myself instead. Sin, you can't be hiding shit from Beast at a time like this. Something could happen to you and nobody would know! Floyd is about to go on the warpath and there's no telling who he will go after. Be smart about what you do. If Beast questions me, I don't know shit!"

"Psycho, I can't do anything but swallow whatever comes my way. I can't promise that I will tell Beast my every move, but I'll try my best to include him somehow," I said once we reached my car. "Them niggas shot me! I'm not waiting for y'all to take care of some shit I can damn well handle myself. What were the names of the detectives that took Rodrigo in?"

"Detective Bradley—"

"And Cooper's racist ass! Yeah let me go get this crazy mutha-fucka before he gets his ass in some shit he can't get out of. I'll talk to you later, Psych," I said jumping into my ride. "Those two pigs are crooked as hell and will do anything to pin some shit on him. With his attitude, he would fall right into their trap.

Slamming the door and pushing the button to start the engine, I backed out barely checking my surroundings and zoomed out of the parking lot.

Meesha

Chapter 21
Rodrigo

These hoe ass cops took me to the Grand Crossing police station on 71st and Cottage Grove. I was sitting in a cold ass room with my wrist cuffed to the chair. That was the smartest thing they could've done because if either one of them thought I was going to sing like a songbird, they were sadly mistaken. I wasn't one of those soft ass India Arie ass niggas they were used to.

Detective Cooper stood with his chest poked out as I was manhandled before being shoved in the back of the squad car. He had no idea his days on earth was numbered. Fuck with me, I fuck back harder. No one had been in to say two words to me since they threw my ass in that cold muthafucka. It was all good because my brain was ready for whatever they were trying to come for me with.

The door crept open a little bit and there were low murmurs coming from the other side before it closed again. I already knew bullshit was about to be the entire topic whenever they were ready to face me. Detective Bradley and his side chick Cooper finally entered with a folder in his hand.

"Mr. Vasquez, I hope we didn't have you waiting too long," Cooper smirked. "Hopefully, you were able to get comfortable. You may be here a while. It depends on you."

"Man, let's get on with this shit. I've already wasted too much time as is. You niggas got me held captive in this bitch like I've committed a serious crime when I haven't done a damn thing. Why am I here anyway?" At that point, I was aggravated because Cooper tried taunting me but I was an unbothered nigga.

"We want to ask a couple questions about a string of murders that has taken place since your brother's death," Bradley stated as he shifted in his seat. "Most of those murders took place on the westside of the city and the victims were people that you are known to associate with."

"I'm going to make something very clear. Sosa is not present in this room, Detective Bradley," I said with a smile. The look on his face was priceless if I say so myself.

Sifting through some of the papers in the folder, Bradley glanced up at me as he slid a photocopy of a mugshot toward me. "This is you, correct?"

"It looks a lot like me but my name ain't Sosa. If you want to question his ass, it may be awhile before he returns because he's on vacation at the moment. I'm standing in for him as he rests up and get his mind right. Losing Max took a toll on him mentally, he's coping with that shit in his own way."

"Sosa, I'm not in the mood for your bullshit right now. Enough of the games, Buddy!" Cooper belted out.

"Do I look like I play games, Cooper? You know I don't, that's why I'm sitting here chained to a fuckin' chair! Now I *said* Sosa ain't in this muthafucka! For the record, we are not buddies, nigga. I don't clique up with the law."

Copper opened his mouth to respond but Bradley stop him beforehand. "Okay," he said giving his partner a death stare. "Mr. Vasquez, what do you know about your brother's murder?"

"The only thing I know about my brother's murder is the fact that he's no longer walking these streets with me. My question to you is, what steps is being made to find out who made that happen?"

"You don't ask the fucking questions, we do, Boy!" Cooper yelled.

"Do you use the same tone with yo' muthafuckin' son? I bet the lil bastard rules the fuck outta yo' soft ass. Direct that shit towards him before he be the one to shoot yo' ass while you sleep. You got one more time to use those hillbilly ass words in reference to me. Don't believe me? Try that shit again once I'm no longer cuffed to this chair."

"Nothing is getting accomplished with the two of you going at each other's throats! Lower the testosterone in this room. We are not here to determine whose dick is bigger, lives were lost in the streets and I want to know who the hell's behind them all!" Bradley yelled.

"That's a no brainer, mine is definitely bigger but that's neither here nor there. Check ya patna because I will continue to react accordingly when he comes at me like I'm one of his kids. He needs a do over at training camp to learn how to defuse a situation. Better yet, he needs an extracurricular course on communication. He's the one that's being a dick, direct your anger his way."

Sighing loudly, Bradley shuffled the papers that he'd scattered on the table before he continued his line of questioning. "What happened at the cemetery last week?"

"We buried my brother," I said hunching my shoulder.

"I know your brother was laid to rest. Who was shooting at you and your family?"

"Wasn't nobody shooting at us. I don't know what you're talking about. There was no shooting while I was present," I replied nonchalantly.

"After your debut on the Channel Nine news, we went to the very cemetery and recovered plenty of gun shells not too far from your brother's gravesite. You mean to tell me there wasn't a shootout?" he asked.

"That's exactly what I'm saying. Maybe the muthafuckas that killed my brother went back to try to kill him again. Shit, I don't know."

"Why did you feel the need to go on live television and say the things you said? Was it just for show?"

"Nah, I meant everything I said on that broadcast. One thing I didn't do was confirm there was a shooting that took place. What I did address was my family being exploited for a story when their murderers were still roaming around free. I have a problem knowing there's not one cop actually trying to find out who killed them!"

"That's not true. We are trying our best to find the culprits, but we need your help. We have suspicions that Floyd and his crew is involved somehow. We also know that you and your brother Mauricio is out for revenge as well."

"How the hell you figure that? Oh, because of who my father was? Get the fuck outta here with that bullshit, man. You don't know shit and you can stop fishing. I don't fuck with Floyd and I have no clue what he has going on."

"James Carter is your guardian, right?" Cooper finally found his voice to ask.

"That nigga ain't never had guardianship over me!"

A light tap on the door interrupted what I was saying and a uniformed officer appeared in the doorway. Detective Bradley turned toward him with a heated expression on his face. "I'm in the middle of an interrogation! What is it?" he exclaimed.

"There's a—" before he could finish his sentence, he was shoved to the side and in walked Sin.

Both Bradley and Cooper looked like they'd seen a ghost but within seconds Coopers facial expression turned into a scowl.

"Is my client under arrest?" Sin asked calmly.

"No but—"

"Good, enough said. Uncuff him, this interrogation is over!" Sin said cutting Bradley off.

"We're not finished questioning him, Miss Walker," Cooper sneered standing to his feet.

"That's not my problem. If my client isn't under arrest, he will not sit here a minute longer. Had he been given the opportunity to make a phone call, you wouldn't have gotten as far as you did in your line of questioning. Cooper it's been awhile since I've conducted any type of business with you, but I'm still the black bitch you remember. Uncuff Mr. Vasquez, now!" Sin hissed.

Cooper didn't attempt to move and he and Sin stared each other down intensely. Bradley on the other hand, stood from his seat and walked around the table as he unhooked his keys from his belt. The clinking sound alerted Cooper to what he was about to do.

"You don't have to listen to this, bitch!" Cooper roared. "She doesn't even practice law anymore, fuck her! There's no way she's taking him out of our custody."

"Copper, I see you're still a bitter ass, racist muthafucka. I'd advise you to watch the shit that you say about me. I'll sue you as well as the department faster than you could pull your dick out to piss. I still practice law, look me up. But I can't say the same about your badge once I get it snatched from under your ass," she smirked.

"Kiss my ass, Sincere. I would never lose my job behind you, black bitch!

"Cooper! Shut the fuck up for God's sake!" Bradley bellowed while unlocking the cuffs. "You're free to leave," he mumbled. Rubbing my wrist where the cuff had been, I stood as I glared at Cooper. The urge to knock him on his ass was strong. I knew if I carried out what I really wanted to do I'd be going to lockup for sure. Waltzing over to where Sin was, she motioned for me to leave the room. Getting out of that room was like a breath of fresh air.

"I got my eye on you, Boy!" Cooper snapped as I crossed the threshold.

My legs stopped moving instantly and I was pushed hard in my back. I swung around angrily coming face to face with Sin. "Don't feed into that shit, keep moving!" Doing as I was told, I turned and walked down the hall without another word with Sin hot on my heels. What did they say to you in there, Rodrigo? I hope you didn't say anything to incriminate yourself."

"You know me better than that, Sin. They tried hard to blame the murders of those westside niggas on me and Ricio. Supposedly, we are out for revenge but they have no proof of that. I really pissed Cooper off back there," I laughed.

"Cooper and Bradley are going to be all over your ass, especially Cooper. Rodrigo, you're going to have to move like you don't exist. I don't know how you'll pull it off, but make it happen," Sin said as we entered her car. "Where are you going? Never mind, I'm taking your half breed ass home and you better not leave for the rest of the night," she said backing out of the parking spot.

"Your name is not Maritza, Sin."

"Nigga, I'm the closest thing to her! Say something else so I can slap the shit outta you," she said without taking her eyes off the road.

I knew not to push her buttons because she was pissed at the way Cooper came at her. But I heard what she said as she preached to me. Sin had given me the green light to kill without saying it directly.

Meesha

Chapter 22
Big Jim

Latorra still hadn't been back to work and she wasn't answering my calls. In fact, I didn't know if she blocked me or not after receiving the email about the test results. My suspicions were correct, I am her father. Learning the truth made a nigga happy as hell, but the real reason behind knowing was why I was beyond excited. My plan to get at Ricio and his muthafuckin' brother was about to be put in play.

I had to figure out how to bring this nigga up in a conversation with Latorra first. She already had the thought in her mind that I was on some shady shit, and I was. I was laying in my bunk when I felt my phone vibrating under the skimpy ass pillow that was under my head. Hurrying to answer, I saw it was Floyd calling.

"What up?" I said when I connected the call.

"Get yourself ready, I'll be there in time for your visit," he said dolefully.

"Why the hell you sound so sad, nigga?"

"We'll talk about it when I get there. Don't miss this visit, Big."

"Nigga, if you get here with some bullshit news, I'm going to the hole today. Know that!" I said hanging up on his punk ass.

Swinging my legs over the edge of the bunk, I planted my feet on top of my shoes as I dialed Latorra's number again. This time her phone rang until the voicemail picked up. That let me now she didn't block me, she just didn't answer. I didn't have time to fuck with her right then because I had to stash my phone before I left for my visit. As I got dressed, my cellie entered as I pulled a shirt over my head.

"Hey, Big can I borrow one of your honey buns?"

"Nigga, why you always beggin'! All you do is walk around this muthafucka wit yo' hand held out. I'm not about to be taking care of yo' ass around this muthafucka! You better sign up for a job or get yo' ass on that tablet and finesse a bitch so she can hold you down while you in here," I said frowning at him.

"Man, you didn't have to say all that shit—"

"Yes, the fuck I did because if I didn't, you wouldn't know how the fuck I really felt, nigga! I'm an outspoken muthafucka and you've known this from day one. Ain't shit changed. Hell nawl, you can't have nothing that belongs to me!"

He had an attitude and walked out with his stomach still on empty. I didn't give a damn about his feelings, there was more important shit I had to worry about. As soon as I hid my phone, a guard entered my cell. I quickly acted like I was organizing my clothes and glanced over my shoulder.

"Carter, you have a visitor."

Rising to my full height, I was fuming. "How many times do I have to tell you not to walk in my shit without letting your presence be known? Y'all want us to respect y'all, but we don't get the same in return," I hissed.

"I'm just doing my job. I was sent to get you for visit, that's all. The rest of the noise you can keep. It's either you want to go for visit or not, it doesn't matter to me," he said.

The guard was one I'd never seen before. He was muscled up like a fuckin' wrestler but I knew I could drop his ass in a minute. Slamming the door to my storage bin, I followed the Big Show out onto the Block. He led me to the visitation room and I spotted Floyd sitting at a table by the window and he was high as fuck. His ass must've faked the funk until he was allowed inside because the warden didn't play that shit around there.

"You on that shit, fam?" I asked as I sat down.

"What?" he asked looking dumbfounded. "Naw, there's so much going on and I'm tired." He rubbed his nose a couple times and ran his hand down his face.

Leaning across the table while pressing firmly on my elbows, I looked him in his eyes. "Nigga, I've been selling drugs for years and I know what a muthafuckin' junkie looks like when I see one. That's the reason my shit crumbling to the ground and you can't run it the way I taught yo' ass," I scowled.

"Big, I swear I'm just tired," he lied with a straight face.

"The very eyes that you're looking at me with, are the same ones that's telling me you're high," I snarled grabbing him by his already wrinkled shirt. "Your eyes are glazed and dilated like a muthafucka, Floyd. What the fuck is going on?"

"Carter!" a guard screamed.

"Aight, man damn!" I shot back as I shoved Floyd and released him. "Start talking, nigga."

"Big, since you got knocked, a lot of shit fell on me. everything was good until the truth about Reese surfaced. After that hit the fan, things have gone from sugar to shit. I'm gon' be honest you, I started fuckin' with snow to keep my sanity. You act like I'm strung out, but I'm not. I have it under control."

"Obviously, you don't if my whole westside crew is fuckin' dead! Ain't shit under control, including you. With all the chaos going on, I can only imagine how my money is lookin'. I won't take yo' word on that because you won't tell the truth about how much of my shit you personally put up your nose. What else haven't you informed me about?"

Floyd glanced around the room with beads of sweat forming on his forehead. The way his Adam's apple bobbed up and down told me he was nervous. He cleared his throat repeatedly while snorting like the cokehead he was and his stalling was starting to piss me off.

"Speak now or forever hold your muthafuckin' peace, bitch! It shouldn't take you this long to state facts, Floyd. Don't make me fuck you up in this muthafucka."

"Um, Money is dead. His body was found in a dumpster on 147th in the forest preserve."

"Explain how every time you report back to me, it's always one of ours that's lying in the morgue. We have never lost so many soldiers during a war. In the short amount of time we've been at odds with these niggas, we've lost too many to count!" I said banging my fist on the table.

"Carter, that's my last warning. The next outburst and your visit will end abruptly," the guard yelled. If he knew what I know he'd shut the fuck up. The way my temper was raging, I didn't give a fuck.

"It wasn't my fault. I sent him to get Ricio's girl and he fucked up somewhere."

"Why was he the one doing your dirty work? You were supposed to be the muthafucka going after her, not him. That's what you had me believing the last time we spoke. If you keep your nose out of the product, maybe you can do your damn job," I shot back at his ass.

"Something came up and I gave him strict instructions that he didn't follow. They never listen and go about things their own way. Shake died behind carelessness, now I have to live with that for the rest of my life! You don't think I'm worried? I could be next, nigga."

"Shake died, when?" I asked gripping the edge of the table.

"Last week. He flat lined right in front of me, Big. The doctors did all they could but he couldn't hold on."

"And you didn't tell me this because?"

"I didn't—"

Before I could stop myself, I leaped over the table and started fucking him up. My fist connected with every part of his face and I drew blood immediately. Floyd fell out of the chair and onto the floor. I followed him and continued whooping his ass. Everything was happening because of his lack of leadership.

I was grabbed from behind and pulled off him by one of the guards. I wasn't pulled back far enough so I took the opportunity to kick that nigga square in the face. The impact wasn't to my liking so I threw an elbow at the guard and he released the hold he had around my waist. I made my move and started stomping that nigga like Caine did ole boy in *Menace to Society*.

"Get some help over here," I heard before I was shocked with a taser. My body convulsed before I fell to the floor in pain. My nerves were nonexistent and I had no feeling in my legs. "Help me get his ass to solitary and get this nigga some help. He beat the fuck out of him."

I was hoisted up by two people but I couldn't even open my eyes to see who they were. My legs felt like noodles and I was unable to walk so I was dragged to my destination with my feet sliding along the floor. Trying to lift my head was a chore because it was heavy as hell.

"Put his ass in lucky number thirteen. He needs time to himself to think about what he just did back there. We should've beat his ass like he beat the fuck out of that stupid nigger." Throwing me inside on the cold concrete floor, the metal door was slammed and I was left alone with my thoughts.

Beating the fuck out of Floyd added more time to my prison stay but it was worth it. His ass was fucking up my establishment anyway so what the fuck did it matter. I didn't know what was really going on out in the street anyway because my right-hand man was holding back on too much shit. He'd better pray I never see the light of day because he'd be a dead muthafucka.

***

I woke up vaguely remembering the incident that landed me in solitary confinement. Lying on the cold floor with my body aching, I used the light that beamed into the small room from the window. There was a cot, toilet and a sink in the room, nothing else. I wish I hadn't let my anger get the best of me.

Beating Floyd's ass was something I didn't regret and remorse was something I didn't feel. His ass had one job and that was to run my shit. He couldn't even do that correctly. I've been in prison for an entire year and I was ready to take my black ass home. Rod's ass hadn't answered his phone to discuss my case in a week.

Now that I'm locked down by myself, there would be no way for me to try to contact him again until after I was put back on the Block. Me being the OG that I was, I would rock it out for the time being. It wasn't like I had much of a choice. Hearing the sound of keys clinking together, the small slot in the door opened and I saw a pair of eyes peeking inside.

"Mr. Carter?" A soft voice filled the room as it echoed off the walls. "Are you alright?"

I recognized the voice immediately and I jumped up and went to the slot. On the other side Latorra was kneeling down to look inside. "Yeah, I'm good. How did you know I was here?"

"I've been assigned to this post today. I was told to come check on you to make sure you were still breathing. My job is done, I'll add my findings to your notes. Keep your head up in here," she said as she raised up.

"Latorra," I said lowly so only she could hear me. "Don't treat me like one of these prisoners, dammit! Talk to me."

"You are one of these prisoners," she said lowering herself back down looking into the slot. I won't jeopardize my job by discussing my personal life with you. We found out the truth and now it's back to the regularly scheduled program. There's no way for us to build any type of relationship while you're behind these walls. I have bills to pay. Good day, Carter," she said making a move to stand.

"If you get yo' ass up and walk away I will make sure you stop breathing the moment you drive away from this prison! Daughter or not. I'm your father and you will do as I say!"

"Are you threatening me?"

"I don't make threats, only promises. Don't believe me, try me. You live 7973 S. Aberdeeen Street in a two-flat building on the second floor. You won't ever sleep soundly if you cross me, Latorra."

Her eyes widen when I spit her address at her and the fear was profound. At that moment I didn't give a fuck because I had a job for her to do and she needed to get with the program. She had Carter blood running through her veins and she was about to be one grimy bitch with her father's help.

"I haven't had a father my whole life and just because a test proved you to be that missing piece in my life, doesn't mean I have to do as you say. I'm a grown woman that's been on her own for years, fuck you! I don't need yo' ass for shit. By the way, I don't care if you know where I live, I'm not worried."

"You should be worried to be honest," I laughed. Here is what you will do. Find out what Ricio is up to since his brother's passing. I need to know where he eats, sleeps, shits, and fuck. Meaning, I want his location. Don't try to tell me you don't know because a little birdie already told me you're fucking the nigga. Have some information for me the next time I see you, Latorra."

"Ricio? What the hell do you need information on him for?" she asked angrily.

Yeah, she had feelings for the muthafucka but that shit was about to be tested big time. "That's not your concern. I want you to concentrate on getting as much information out of that nigga as possible. Find out about his brother too. You did know he had another brother, right? Or are you his little secret?"

"Fuck you, Carter! I'm not doing shit and I hope you rot in this muthafucka! I'll make sure of it by going to the warden letting him know that you have been threatening me. How about I throw in a little lie about you coming on to me sexually too, nigga. Kiss my ass with yo' punk ass."

"You may not want to do that, daughter. I'm in jail, Toots, not dead. Money talks around this bitch and I can get the word out on the street. Don't test me," I snarled.

"I don't even talk to Ricio anymore, he has a girlfriend."

"Well find a way to befriend her ass to get to him! You have until the end of the week to bring me back something that will help me or you will be in a world of trouble. I don't give a fuck if you gotta throw that ass in a circle, get it done! Now, *you* enjoy the rest of your day, Smith.'

I stood and went back to the piece of shit they called a bed and sat down. Latorra was still peeking through the slot but I was done talking at that point. If she didn't come back with any information for me, I was going to make sure her life got turned upside down and she was going to have a hard time righting it.

Meesha

Chapter 23
Nija

Finding out I was pregnant had my mind in a bad place. I had been thinking about what I wanted to do about this pregnancy since I found out last week. With everything that's been going on between Ricio and I, an abortion was at the forefront of my mind. If that was the route I went with, I would have to travel far away so he wouldn't know about it.

Ricio made it very clear for me not to get an abortion. When I called my doctor first thing Monday morning, she insisted I come in. My pregnancy was confirmed after I demanded three different tests. I was four weeks along. Dr. Hayes was happy because she has been my doctor since I was a teenager and she was like family. Needless to say, her happiness didn't rub off on me. I still had a decision to make and it was leaning toward getting rid of the baby.

"Are you going to sleep in your office tonight?" Tangie my coworker asked from the doorway.

Glancing at the clock on my desk, it was a quarter after five. "Shit, time flies when you have too much on your mind. Thanks, Tangie, I appreciate ya," I said gathering the folders I would need to go over.

"No problem. You want to get something to eat so you can talk about what's on your mind?"

"We can go out to eat but no offense, you know I don't discuss my personal business with coworkers," I laughed. "We are cool as long as we're at work. We haven't established any type of friendship beyond that."

"Tonight, is the night for us to see if we will have a friendship outside of the Department of Human Services. I'll be waiting out front, I need a cigarette," she said pushing off the doorframe.

It didn't take me long to pack up my briefcase and shut down the computer. As I strolled through the empty halls of the building, I wished it was quiet around there all the time. But that was wishful thinking on my part because the place that pays could be a zoo.

Pushing the handle to exit the building, I walked right into a cloud of Tangie's stinky smoke.

Becoming instantly nauseated, I found the nearest flower plant and threw up my lunch from earlier. This baby was really showing out. I rarely vomited because I hated it. Now that the little bean was planted in my uterus, it was part of my daily routine, especially at night.

"Are you okay?" Tangie asked rubbing my back as I spit out the sour taste in my mouth.

Her smoke hit my nostrils again and bile rushed my throat once again. Not able to speak as a stream of vomited shot out of my mouth, I pushed her away the best I could. I guess she thought I was trying to ask for a napkin or something because she placed a couple Kleenex in my hand. After wiping my mouth and spitting one more time, I searched my purse for the mouthwash that had become my best friend.

"Put your cigarette out, Tangie. It's making me sick."

"Since when? You have never complained about my smoke before. Even though you don't smoke, we still come outside to talk about the ratchet bitches that come through here," she said taking another puff but blew the smoke away from me. "Wait a damn minute. Are you pregnant?" she asked excitedly.

"Yeah, I found out last week but don't tell anyone."

"Oh shit! We are definitely going out now to celebrate. Congratulations, Nija! I think you would be a great mother. I see how you be talking to these young mothers in here. Shid, I be taking your advice too sometimes."

"Thank you. Where do you want to go eat? I'm starving," I said adjusting my briefcase strap on my shoulder.

"Applebee's on 95th?" she asked uncertainly.

"Sure, why not. It's on me, I still have a twenty-five-dollar gift card in my purse from three years ago. I'll trail you," I said heading to my car.

"Okay, cool."

The commute to the Applebee's wasn't too bad. The traffic heading west on 95th was not as congested for a Wednesday evening. Tangie drove like a madman that was ready to kill. It was hard keeping up with her so I drove for me and everyone else and let her go ahead. When I pulled up to the restaurant, she was already parked smoking yet, another cigarette.

I parked beside her and waited until she finished messing up her lungs before I got out. We walked into the restaurant together and were seated immediately. Once our drink orders were taken, Tangie started planning a baby shower for me out loud.

"We can have little blue or pink cupcakes, lots of beautiful decorations and balloons. We can have a gender reveal party!" she blared excitedly.

"Shhh! You're too loud," I hissed.

Tangie looked at me and her smile turned into a frown. "Nija, you're not happy about this pregnancy, are you?"

I didn't want to get into why I wasn't happy so I answered her short and sweetly. "No, I'm not and I don't want to talk about it," I said taking a sip from my glass of water with lemon.

"We don't have to. Being a mother is everything, Nija. I am a mother of one and I wouldn't trade my daughter for the world. Now, her funky ass daddy, that's another story. I upgraded from his nothing ass a long time ago. When we ended our relationship, he ended things with our child too.

If I wasn't fucking, he didn't plan on supporting. I had to stop that shit before it started because I wasn't about to subject myself to having sex in order for him to take care of his daughter. There was a time he came to my home and thought he was going to sleep in my bed just to spend the night with his child. Let's say that was the last time I saw him. He signed over his rights. My daughter was still a baby and won't remember any of that shit."

"Damn that's sad. I'm glad you didn't fall for that bullshit. I hate hearing the stories of young women being left to take care of babies they didn't make alone. It goes to show, you have to be careful who you lay down with," I replied.

"I would never purposely put myself in a situation like that. Little boys in grown men bodies have a way of showing you what they want you to see then change up when shit gets real. I had to grow up and take charge of my life because it wasn't about me anymore. My husband came along and changed my life for the better and I'm grateful for all he has done for both of us. He may not be her daddy biologically, but can't nobody say he's not a damn good father to her."

"I know that's right. Every young woman out here isn't so lucky. It's part of the reason I love what I do for a living. I also hate it at the same time because some of those females I want to strangle," I laughed.

"Tell me about it," Tangie agreed.

"Are you ladies ready to order?" the waiter asked walking up to our table.

"Yes, I would like the loaded chicken fajita bowl with extra chicken, hold the bacon and guacamole. Do you guys have strawberry lemonade?" I asked.

"Yes, we do."

"I'll have one of those too, please," I said handing him my menu.

"No problem. What about you ma'am?" he asked Tangie.

"This is on a separate check. I will have—"

"I told you dinner was on me, Tangie," I said cutting her off.

"Girl, your twenty-five-dollar limit will not cover what I'm about to order. I missed lunch today and a bitch 'bouts to eat!" she said looking back down at the menu. "For starters I would like the spinach artichoke dip and also the Bourbon Street steak with extra onions and mushrooms. Garlic mashed potatoes, the four-cheese mac and cheese for the side, and a swirled strawberry frozen lemonade."

"Damn, are you pregnant?" I laughed.

"Hell nawl, I'm not pregnant," Tangie said closing the menu and handing it to the waiter. "Thank you."

"I will be back with your dip and drinks shortly."

"When I'm hungry, I eat. There's no limits when it comes to food," Tangie said continuing where she left off. "It's the second to the last thing I like to do with my mouth."

"Lawd, I don't want to know what the first thing is," I laughed.

"You are a pretty laid-back person outside of work. I'm gonna be honest with you, I thought you were stuck up. Let me explain," she said holding up her hand. "When you started working with us, you came off like you were better than everyone. You wouldn't talk to anyone and you kept to yourself. After time passed, you started to relax and mingle a bit more. But yeah, that's what I thought the first time I saw you."

"Well I'm glad you think differently today. Or do you?"

"Girl bye. That was old shit that I thought you should know. I actually do think differently because you have matured and mastered your craft right before my eyes. That's why I was surprised when you got suspended last week. That shit was foul and I told Vera what I thought too."

"Thanks for at least trying to speak on my behalf, but my sister ain't shit. She knew what the fuck she was doing but it's all good. I needed a couple days away from that place we call work," I said as I heard my phone ringing in my purse.

"Hello," I said when I finally found it.

"Hey baby mama. How are you?" Ricio replied.

"Don't call me that bullshit. What is it?"

"I was calling to check on you. As a matter of fact, I'm coming down the street about to pull up at Kimmie's house."

"She should be there, because I'm not," I said as the waiter set up his little stand with one hand while holding a large tray full of me and Tangie's food.

"Who had the loaded fajita?" the waiter asked.

"I did," I replied while holding the phone. My food was placed in front of me and I was starving. The aroma alone was tantalizing my taste buds.

"Nija where the fuck is you and who are you with?" Ricio yelled into the phone.

"I'll be right back. I have to take this call," I said knowing it would piss him off because his first thought would be on another nigga. Standing from my seat, I left the restaurant. "Ricio, I am trying to eat, what do you want?"

"Answer my question, Nija. Who are you with?"

"Does it really matter? We are not together so what I do should not concern you, Ricio."

"There you go talking stupid again. As long as you're carrying my seed and long after, you will be my concern. You have been my concern for almost a decade and you think it will stop now. Where you at?" he replied heatedly.

"I'm not telling you where I am so you can come show your ass. Go in the house and talk to Kimmie. I'm going back inside to finish eating. You already got me standing outside being rude to my dinner date. I'll call you when I get to the house," I said hanging up before he could start talking shit.

As I walked back into the restaurant, my phone rang and it was Ricio again. I sent him to voicemail continuing on my way back to the table. Tangie was smashing her food making my stomach hurt by watching her eat from several plates.

"Slow down before you choke," I laughed sitting my phone on the table.

"Girl this shit is good, you should try these mash potatoes," she said with a mouthful of food.

"Nah, I'm good. Enjoy them though," I said scooping up my fajita. It didn't take long before I was looking like Tangies twin sister by the mouth. That's how good the delectable dish was. My phone started ringing again and I silenced it without even looking to see who the caller was. It rang two more times back to back and I let it ring.

"Nija, you're not going to answer your phone?" Tangie asked as she sipped her frozen drink?

I shook my head no and kept eating. Ricio would have to understand that we were not in the same place we were for years. I don't have to answer his calls the way I did before. He was going to be mad, but we were playing by my rules now. His rules didn't work for us so it was my turn to lay down a foundation.

Waving down the waiter, I waited patiently until he came over. "I want to order another loaded fajita to go as well as another lemonade."

"No problem, I will get that order in for you. Anything else for you ma'am?" he asked Tangie.

"No thanks," was all she could say as she shoved more food in her mouth.

An hour later we were fat and full trying to force ourselves to finish warm dark chocolate brownies drizzled with hot fudge and vanilla ice cream on the side. The waiter returned carrying the to go meal I ordered and our checks. Placing the gift card and my debit card in the card holder, I handed it to him.

"Use the gift card first and put the remaining balance on my card please." I said as Tangie handed hers back as well and we went back to eating our brownies. "I can't eat anymore. If u invite me out to eat again, make it a month from now. I'm eating for two but I'm not trying to be big as a house."

"I eat like this often. My metabolism is through the roof," Tangie said reaching over for the rest of my brownie. "I'm trying to gain weight but it never happens. I guess it's above me now," she said laughing at the popular hashtag that was making it's way around social media.

"You are crazy," I chuckled digging in my purse. Placing a ten-dollar bill on the table I was ready to go. The waiter came back shortly after with our cards in hand. We both signed the receipts, thanked him and left the restaurant. "I had a good time. Thank you for inviting me out."

"I did too and you're welcome. Give me a call sometime, I'm always trying to get away from the family. There's nothing like a girl's night out every now and again."

"I'll keep that in mind. Drive safely and I'll see you tomorrow."

Getting in my car, I picked up my phone and went through my call log. I had several missed calls but only one was from Ricio. All the others were from Kimmie.

"He got my best friend all riled up for nothing," I said out loud. I noticed I had a voicemail and I decided to check it. I usually let them sit there without listening but something told me to press the play button. Ricio's voice filled the car as I listened on speaker.

"Nija, I don't know how many times I have to tell you that shit is crazy out here in these streets. I need to know where you are at all times not because I'm trying to keep up with you, but because muthafuckas are stupid. You are not the only person I have to worry about, my baby is part of that equation now. It is my duty to protect the both of y'all and you are being stubborn about that shit."

The sound of him opening his car door and slamming it shut was heard loud and clear.

"I'll be here at the house waiting for you to come home. You can try to avoid seeing me, but I'll wait as long as it takes. I love you even if you don't believe I do. I've always loved you, Nija Foster and I always will. Oh shit!"

My eyebrows furrowed as I listening to the screeching of tires followed by a stream of gunshots.

BOC! BOC! BOC! BOC! BOC! BOC! BOC! BOC! BOC! BOC!

"Ricio! Rico! Talk to me baby. Please let me know that you're okay!" I screamed into the phone forgetting it was a recorded message.

"You's a dead muthafucka now, nigga!" I heard a voice yell out as the car peeled away from the scene.

To Be Continued…
Renegade Boys 4
Coming Soon

Submission Guideline

Submit the first three chapters of your completed manuscript to ldpsubmissions@gmail.com, subject line: Your book's title. The manuscript must be in a .doc file and sent as an attachment. Document should be in Times New Roman, double spaced and in size 12 font. Also, provide your synopsis and full contact information. If sending multiple submissions, they must each be in a separate email.

Have a story but no way to send it electronically? You can still submit to LDP/Ca$h Presents. Send in the first three chapters, written or typed, of your completed manuscript to:

LDP: Submissions Dept
Po Box 870494
Mesquite, Tx 75187

DO NOT send original manuscript. Must be a duplicate.

Provide your synopsis and a cover letter containing your full contact information.

Thanks for considering LDP and Ca$h Presents.

Coming Soon from Lock Down Publications/Ca$h Presents

BOW DOWN TO MY GANGSTA

By **Ca$h**

TORN BETWEEN TWO

By **Coffee**

BLOOD STAINS OF A SHOTTA **III**

By **Jamaica**

RENEGADE BOYS IV

By Meesha

STEADY MOBBIN **III**

By **Marcellus Allen**

BLOOD OF A BOSS **VI**

SHADOWS OF THE GAME II

By **Askari**

LOYAL TO THE GAME **IV**

LIFE OF SIN **III**

By **T.J. & Jelissa**

A DOPEBOY'S PRAYER **II**

By **Eddie "Wolf" Lee**

IF LOVING YOU IS WRONG... **III**

By **Jelissa**

TRUE SAVAGE **VII**

By **Chris Green**

BLAST FOR ME **III**

DUFFLE BAG CARTEL **IV**

HEARTLESS GOON

By **Ghost**

ADDICTIED TO THE DRAMA **III**

By **Jamila Mathis**

A HUSTLER'S DECEIT III
KILL ZONE **II**
BAE BELONGS TO ME III
SOUL OF A MONSTER II
By **Aryanna**
THE COST OF LOYALTY **III**
By **Kweli**
A GANGSTER'S SYN II
By **J-Blunt**
KING OF NEW YORK V
RISE TO POWER III
COKE KINGS III
By **T.J. Edwards**
GORILLAZ IN THE BAY IV
De'Kari
THE STREETS ARE CALLING II
Duquie Wilson
KINGPIN KILLAZ IV
STREET KINGS III
PAID IN BLOOD II
Hood Rich
SINS OF A HUSTLA II
ASAD
TRIGGADALE III
Elijah R. Freeman
MARRIED TO A BOSS III
By Destiny Skai & Chris Green
KINGZ OF THE GAME IV
Playa Ray
SLAUGHTER GANG III

BORN HEARTLESS

By Willie Slaughter

THE HEART OF A SAVAGE II

By Jibril Williams

FUK SHYT II

By Blakk Diamond

THE DOPEMAN'S BODYGAURD II

By Tranay Adams

TRAP GOD

By Troublesome

YAYO

By S. Allen

GHOST MOB

Stilloan Robinson

KINGPIN DREAMS

By Paper Boi Rari

Available Now

RESTRAINING ORDER **I & II**

By **CA$H & Coffee**

LOVE KNOWS NO BOUNDARIES **I II & III**

By **Coffee**

RAISED AS A GOON I, II, III & IV

BRED BY THE SLUMS I, II, III

BLAST FOR ME I & II

ROTTEN TO THE CORE I II III

A BRONX TALE I, II, III

DUFFEL BAG CARTEL I II III

By **Ghost**

<u>LAY IT DOWN</u> **I & II**

<u>LAST OF A DYING BREED</u>

<u>BLOOD STAINS OF A SHOTTA I & II</u>

By **Jamaica**

<u>LOYAL TO THE GAME</u>

<u>LOYAL TO THE GAME II</u>

<u>LOYAL TO THE GAME III</u>

<u>LIFE OF SIN I, II</u>

By **TJ & Jelissa**

<u>BLOODY COMMAS I & II</u>

<u>SKI MASK CARTEL I II & III</u>

<u>KING OF NEW YORK I II,III IV</u>

<u>RISE TO POWER I II</u>

<u>COKE KINGS I II</u>

By **T.J. Edwards**

<u>IF LOVING HIM IS WRONG…I & II</u>

<u>LOVE ME EVEN WHEN IT HURTS I II III</u>

By **Jelissa**

<u>WHEN THE STREETS CLAP BACK I & II III</u>

By **Jibril Williams**

<u>A DISTINGUISHED THUG STOLE MY HEART I II & III</u>

<u>LOVE SHOULDN'T HURT I II III IV</u>

<u>RENEGADE BOYS I II III</u>

By **Meesha**

<u>A GANGSTER'S CODE I &, II III</u>

<u>A GANGSTER'S SYN</u>

By **J-Blunt**

<u>PUSH IT TO THE LIMIT</u>

By **Bre' Hayes**

BLOOD OF A BOSS **I, II, III, IV, V**

SHADOWS OF THE GAME

By **Askari**

THE STREETS BLEED MURDER **I, II & III**

THE HEART OF A GANGSTA I II& III

By **Jerry Jackson**

CUM FOR ME

CUM FOR ME 2

CUM FOR ME 3

CUM FOR ME 4

CUM FOR ME 5

An **LDP Erotica Collaboration**

BRIDE OF A HUSTLA **I II & II**

THE FETTI GIRLS **I, II& III**

CORRUPTED BY A GANGSTA I, II III, IV

BLINDED BY HIS LOVE

By **Destiny Skai**

WHEN A GOOD GIRL GOES BAD

By **Adrienne**

THE COST OF LOYALTY I II

By Kweli

A GANGSTER'S REVENGE **I II III & IV**

THE BOSS MAN'S DAUGHTERS

THE BOSS MAN'S DAUGHTERS II

THE BOSSMAN'S DAUGHTERS III

THE BOSSMAN'S DAUGHTERS IV

THE BOSS MAN'S DAUGHTERS **V**

A SAVAGE LOVE **I & II**

BAE BELONGS TO ME I II

A HUSTLER'S DECEIT I, II, III

WHAT BAD BITCHES DO I, II, III

SOUL OF A MONSTER

KILL ZONE

By **Aryanna**

A KINGPIN'S AMBITON

A KINGPIN'S AMBITION **II**

I MURDER FOR THE DOUGH

By **Ambitious**

TRUE SAVAGE

TRUE SAVAGE II

TRUE SAVAGE **III**

TRUE SAVAGE **IV**

TRUE SAVAGE **V**

TRUE SAVAGE **VI**

By **Chris Green**

A DOPEBOY'S PRAYER

By **Eddie "Wolf" Lee**

THE KING CARTEL **I, II & III**

By **Frank Gresham**

THESE NIGGAS AIN'T LOYAL **I, II & III**

By **Nikki Tee**

GANGSTA SHYT **I II &III**

By **CATO**

THE ULTIMATE BETRAYAL

By **Phoenix**

BOSS'N UP **I , II & III**

By **Royal Nicole**

I LOVE YOU TO DEATH

By Destiny J

I RIDE FOR MY HITTA

I STILL RIDE FOR MY HITTA

By **Misty Holt**

LOVE & CHASIN' PAPER

By **Qay Crockett**

TO DIE IN VAIN

SINS OF A HUSTLA

By **ASAD**

BROOKLYN HUSTLAZ

By **Boogsy Morina**

BROOKLYN ON LOCK I & II

By **Sonovia**

GANGSTA CITY

By **Teddy Duke**

A DRUG KING AND HIS DIAMOND I & II III

A DOPEMAN'S RICHES

HER MAN, MINE'S TOO I, II

CASH MONEY HO'S

By Nicole Goosby

TRAPHOUSE KING **I II & III**

KINGPIN KILLAZ I II III

STREET KINGS I II

PAID IN BLOOD

By **Hood Rich**

LIPSTICK KILLAH **I, II, III**

CRIME OF PASSION I & II

By **Mimi**

STEADY MOBBN' **I, II, III**

By **Marcellus Allen**

WHO SHOT YA **I, II, III**

Renta

GORILLAZ IN THE BAY **I II III**

DE'KARI

TRIGGADALE I II

Elijah R. Freeman

GOD BLESS THE TRAPPERS I, II, III

THESE SCANDALOUS STREETS I, II, III

FEAR MY GANGSTA I, II, III

THESE STREETS DON'T LOVE NOBODY I, II

BURY ME A G I, II, III, IV, V

A GANGSTA'S EMPIRE I, II, III, IV

THE DOPEMAN'S BODYGAURD

Tranay Adams

THE STREETS ARE CALLING

Duquie Wilson

MARRIED TO A BOSS… I II

By Destiny Skai & Chris Green

KINGZ OF THE GAME I II III

Playa Ray

SLAUGHTER GANG I II

By Willie Slaughter

THE HEART OF A SAVAGE

By Jibril Williams

FUK SHYT

By Blakk Diamond

DON'T F#CK WITH MY HEART I II

By Linnea

ADDICTED TO THE DRAMA I II

By Jamila

BOOKS BY LDP'S CEO, CA$H

TRUST IN NO MAN

TRUST IN NO MAN 2

TRUST IN NO MAN 3

BONDED BY BLOOD

SHORTY GOT A THUG

THUGS CRY

THUGS CRY 2

THUGS CRY 3

TRUST NO BITCH

TRUST NO BITCH 2

TRUST NO BITCH 3

TIL MY CASKET DROPS

RESTRAINING ORDER

RESTRAINING ORDER 2

IN LOVE WITH A CONVICT

Coming Soon

BONDED BY BLOOD 2

BOW DOWN TO MY GANGSTA

CPSIA information can be obtained
at www.ICGtesting.com
Printed in the USA
LVHW051600071019
633431LV00013B/1062/P